Selena Stared At Luke, Reaching A Decision.

There wasn't a hotel room available for miles around, and he was tired and hungry. She said in a rush, "I'll share my room with you."

Luke wasn't just surprised at her offer—he was stunned. "What did you say?" he asked after his rejoicing senses settled down.

From the look on her face, it was evident that she was reconsidering. "Of course, if you'd rather not . . ." She shrugged as her voice trailed away.

Rather not? Luke would rather not have eaten for a month before dreaming of turning down her offer. "Green Eyes, I may be rude on occasion, but I'm never stupid," he said. "I'd be both grateful and honored to share your room."

"Yes, but will you be good?" she asked with unintentional provocation.

Luke's smile was a study in advanced sensuality. "I'll be more than good," he promised in a tingle-producing murmur. "I'll be terrific."

Dear Reader:

Happy Holidays from all of us at Silhouette Desire! This is our favorite time of year, so we've pulled together a wonderful month of love stories that are our gifts to you, our readers.

We start out with *Man of the Month* Luke Branson in Joan Hohl's *Handsome Devil*, which is also a sequel to *The Gentleman Insists*, February 1989's *Man of the Month*.

Also, look for three wonderful stories filled with the spirit of the season: *Upon A Midnight Clear* by Laura Leone, *The Pendragon Virus* by Cait London and *Glory, Glory* by Linda Lael Miller. Rounding out December are the delightful *Looking For Trouble* by Nancy Martin and the tantalizing *The Bridal Price* by Barbara Boswell. All together, these six books might make great presents for yourself—or perhaps for a loved one!

So enjoy December's Silhouette Desire books. And as for 1991 . . . well, we have some wonderful plans in store—including another year of exciting *Man of the Month* stories! But more on all that in the new year. In the meantime, I wish each and every one of you the warmest seasons greetings.

All the best,

Lucia Macro
Senior Editor

JOAN HOHL

HANDSOME DEVIL

SILHOUETTE *Desire*®

Published by Silhouette Books New York

America's Publisher of Contemporary Romance

SILHOUETTE BOOKS
300 East 42nd St., New York, N.Y. 10017

ISBN: 0-373-05612-5

First Silhouette Books printing December 1990

Printed in the U.S.A.

Books by Joan Hohl

Silhouette Desire

A Much Needed Holiday #247
*Texas Gold #294
*California Copper #312
*Nevada Silver #330
Lady Ice #354
One Tough Hombre #372
Falcon's Flight #390
The Gentleman Insists #475
Christmas Stranger #540
Handsome Devil #612

*Desire trilogy

Silhouette Intimate Moments

Moments Harsh, Moments Gentle #35

Silhouette Special Edition

Thorne's Way #54
Forever Spring #444
Thorne's Wife #537

Silhouette Romance

A Taste for Rich Things #334
Someone Waiting #358
The Scent of Lilacs #376

Silhouette Books

Silhouette Summer Sizzlers 1988
"Grand Illusion"

JOAN HOHL,

a Gemini and an inveterate daydreamer, says she always has her head in the clouds. An avid reader all her life, she discovered romances about ten years ago. "And as soon as I read one," she confesses, "I was hooked." Now an extremely prolific author, she is thrilled to be getting paid for doing exactly what she loves best.

For
Rita Clay Estrada,
Sonny and Jan Reitenauer,
Mick and Bill Hunsberger,
Parris and Ted Bonds
and
Marshall Bonds:
For their shared companionship and
laughter during the Texas research
experience.

One

She had the gleaming black hair and glittering green eyes of a cat . . . or a witch.

Squinting against the rays from the setting sun, Luke Branson studied the woman sitting cross-legged on the flagstone patio opposite him.

He disapproved of her, of this type of woman—confident, independent, flip, supremely able to hold her own with her contemporaries, both male and female. But then, Luke disapproved of most women, whatever their type. He admitted that there were exceptions to the rule, but he was convinced they were few and far between.

Luke had reason for his disapproval and disdain of the feminine gender. One beautiful, seemingly sweet, loving and caring woman had not only put a knife through his heart, twisting it mercilessly into his guts and his mind—she had slashed his soul to dark ribbons of bitterness and loathing. And then she had administered the final, crushing blow by taking his child.

Even after six years, Luke believed his feelings of antipathy for women was viable and valid. But, while disdaining most females over the age of consent, he felt no compunction about using them in the way only he felt they *were* useful—to appease a man's natural hungers.

And this woman, this cat-witch woman, appeared to Luke to be more useful than most in that respect.

Selena McInnes was exquisite—small, delicate, stunning. She appeared fragile, dainty, almost childlike. Her appearance was deceiving.

Her laughter sparkled on the hot, dry air, causing a shiver deep inside Luke. Instead of quenching the heat in a deeper, more vulnerable section of his body, the chill intensified his searing ache.

Damn. Shifting uncomfortably in the plastic webbed lawn chair, Luke cursed in silence and tightened his grip around the icy can in his hand. Raising the beer to his lips, he took a long swallow, but the cold liquid proved unequal to the fire burning in his loins.

He wanted her. In the worst way. In the best way. In every way imaginable. The yearning had begun the first time Luke saw Selena two weeks ago. It had increased by degrees every time he'd seen her since.

And he would have her, Luke vowed, tilting the can for another swig. The only questions in his mind were when and where. The consideration of how he would have her didn't enter into his contemplation—Luke planned to have Selena in every way possible. Whether he could have her at all didn't enter into it, either. Without a shred of conceit, Luke was well aware of his attraction to the opposite sex. In the six years since his divorce, more than one woman had called him a handsome devil, and the words were applicable to both his looks and character. Luke didn't resent the connotations implied. On the contrary, he relished them.

An anticipatory smile softened his hard-looking lips. Behind the shield of sunglasses, his dark eyes glittered with intent as his heated gaze skimmed her small, inviting body.

And Selena presented a great deal of her slender body for his, or anyone else's, inspection. She was dressed—or almost dressed—in what Luke had begun to think of as her daily working uniform of short shorts and a sleeveless cotton knit pullover. The shorts were fire-engine red, the skimpy top was canary yellow. Flat, nylon-strapped sandals lay forgotten next to her oversize denim shoulder bag on the patio floor behind her. Her feet were bare, as were her enticingly curved legs, which appeared incredibly long, considering her height of just under five feet, two inches.

Fanning the flame that flared ever hotter inside him, Luke allowed himself the pleasure of examining the length of Selena's legs, from her trim ankles to her smooth, silky-looking thighs. His gaze, hidden by the dark lenses, paused on the evocative curve of red material covering the gentle mound at the apex of her thighs. Gulping at the warming beer, he dragged his eyes away from the center of his desire. Restless, he looked away only to find himself staring at the swell of her breasts, braless beneath the thin shirt. Like the rest of her, her breasts were small, delicately formed, exquisitely enticing. Luke swallowed the last of his beer after his hot-eyed gaze had devoured the tips of her breasts impudently poking against the soft material of her pullover. Absently crushing the empty can with his fingers, he raised his eyes to her face. His body stilled. His breath caught in his throat. His eyes narrowed behind the smoky glass.

Framed by a waist-long mass of shimmering black hair, Selena's face was stunning. Her features were delicate. Her skin was soft. Her small nose complemented her perfectly-shaped full lips. And, set in her beautiful face, her green eyes held a mysterious depth into which Luke longed to lose himself.

She laughed again. Luke groaned in silent protest. His lips tightened into an unrelenting line of decision. He wanted her laughing mouth, wanted to taste it, ravish it, then suck all the sweetness out of it. And it would have to be soon, or he'd go out of his mind with desire. Frustration eating him alive, Luke tossed the mangled can into the plastic-lined empty oil drum used for trash.

"Another beer, Luke?"

With an odd sense of relief, Luke shifted his attention from the object of his raging passion to the lazily sprawled figure of his host and employer. "Yeah." Luke caught the cold can tossed to him, popped the top, then tilted it in salute. "Thanks, Will."

The older man nodded. "What the hell would we do without beer out here?" he muttered. "Or anywhere else, for that matter?"

Luke grinned, revealing hard, even teeth that flashed startling white in contrast to his sun-bronzed skin. "Get damned thirsty, I suspect," he drawled.

"Right." Will nodded again, emphatically. "I sometimes ask myself what the hell I'm doing out here in this Godforsaken corner of Texas." His sun-weathered face creased in a wide smile. "Other times, I wonder if there's any other place in the world to be."

"I know what you mean." With the murmured comment, Luke transferred his gaze to the purple-hued mountains in the distance. Unlike the forest-covered mountains he was accustomed to in the East, the starkly bare range in the Big Bend fascinated him. The sensation was similar to what he felt for Selena— the impact of both on his senses had been immediate and strong.

However, the impact of the mountains had come almost five months before the impact of the woman.

Like his host and many of the others gathered on the patio of the house overlooking the Rio Grande, Luke was a dropout, burned by life and circumstances.

Turning from the jagged range, now becoming a dark silhouette against the crimson sky of sunset, Luke glanced over the laughing, murmuring group around him. He knew the personal histories of only three of the ten people who had put in an appearance that afternoon, and two of those were sketchy.

Luke's gaze settled on two men lounging against the protective rail rimming the patio. The youngest was in his early twenties. His name was Carlton Ames III, dubbed "The Kid" by Will. The Kid had dropped out of a wealthy environment and away from a smothering mother. He earned enough to survive by waiting tables at a nearby restaurant-bar frequented by the tourists, natives and part-time residents of the tiny community of Study Butte.

The other man was older, tougher looking. Jasper Chance—called "Main" by his friends—a native Texan from Tyler, had dropped out of a lucrative position with a brokerage firm in New York City, burned out by the intensity of the stock exchange. Main now earned his living by managing the general store and stable.

Luke switched his gaze to his host and employer. William Rightmyer was the oldest member of the group. At 54, Will had dropped out of the grueling, fourteen-hour-a-day position as president of a large textile firm in the South. Rich by anybody's standards, Will had purchased a store, the stable managed by Main, the restaurant-bar in which The Kid waited tables, and a river and trail tour business. All of the assembled group worked for Will in one capacity or another, including Luke.

Luke had not dropped out of a mind-burning career, but away from the soul-singeing experience of divorce, followed by losing custody of his daughter to his ex-wife and her wealthy new British husband. Considered by many experts to be one of the leading architects in the world, Luke loved and was still working at his profession. In addition to designing a house he planned to eventually build for himself, Luke occasionally worked the counter at both the general store and the tour office for Will. It was while doing a stint behind the counter of the tour office that he had first met Selena McInnes.

She had strolled into the office as if she owned the place and had been greeted by Will with enthusiasm and undisguised affection.

"I was beginning to think you weren't coming back," Will had barked, swinging the woman into the air before crushing her in a bear hug. "How was South America?"

"Hot, steamy and wild." Selena had laughed and tossed her head, sending her mass of silky black hair swirling around her shoulders—and a dark hunger swirling around Luke's insides. She looked slightly wild herself. He felt an immediate need to taste her wildness.

Will had given her a close, frowning look. "You didn't lose anybody, did you?"

She'd sobered at once. "No. But right before I left, I heard that a group that went down the river the week after I did ran into some trouble. Two were lost."

"Lost?" Luke had asked. "How? I mean...in what way?"

Selena had turned to give him a level stare from her cool green eyes. Her voice was brisk, devoid of emotion. "In the usual way when a raft runs into trouble on a river."

"Drowned?" he demanded.

"Yes." She maintained her aloofness.

"But where were the guides?"

Her coolness thawed in a flash of anger. "One of the men lost was a guide. And who the hell are you?"

Luke was about to tell her, but Will beat him to it. He made the introductions, then gave Luke a brief explanation. "Selena was on a busman's holiday. Went off to explore the rivers in the jungles of South America about a month before you arrived." He draped one arm around her shoulders and grinned at Luke. "Except for the odd jaunts she takes now and again, Lena's been with me for over four years." He transferred his gaze to her and smiled. "She's the best guide I've got."

Now, recalling the shock and amazement he had experienced that afternoon two weeks ago, Luke slid his gaze to her animated face. Unbelievable as it still seemed, this delicate, beautiful woman—who had at once stolen his breath and kicked his libido into overdrive—held the status of expert river-and-trail guide. She had been called upon to rescue numerous tourists who had become lost or hurt while on the trail or the river.

Try as he would, Luke couldn't imagine the small woman rescuing anybody, except perhaps a child. Yet Will had assured Luke that she had, and very capably, too.

Dropping his hooded gaze, Luke was contemplating the possible strength in her delicate shoulders and slim arms when his reverie was broken by a blast of loud music, followed by a brash-voiced command.

"C'mon, Lena, let's show 'em how it's done." The order came from one of the men, a recently hired river guide named Dave, who had evidently had more than his share of the beer. Grabbing one of her hands, he hauled Selena to her feet. "Swing your pretty tush, baby. Rock and roll!"

Laughing, Selena moved with smooth grace into the rhythm.

Brooding, disgruntled, Luke watched her. His pulse thrummed in time with the sensuous gyrations of her lithe body. His throat went bone dry. Parched, he emptied the can with long swallows of beer. As he tossed it into the oil drum, Luke saw several of the others joining in with the two dancers. Eyes narrowed, he watched as Dave, eyes burning with a lascivious light, turned his attention to a tall, ultraslim woman who was undulating across the patio toward him.

Luke knew the woman, they all knew her. Her name was Brenda. She tended bar at Will's place and shared space and the expenses in the small house Selena was buying near the tour office. Brenda had light hair and dark, sleepy-looking eyes, a tiny waist and large, unbelievably high breasts that jiggled enticingly as she moved.

A cynical smile curved Luke's lips as he observed the jiggling woman's effect on Dave, who appeared on the point of salivating. The music suddenly changed to a slow, sultry tempo. Dave pulled Brenda into his arms. Left alone, Selena closed her eyes and swayed to the evocative music.

Reacting to impulse, Luke stood and walked to her. A dreamy smile feathered over her soft mouth when he slid his hands around her waist. But her dreamy expression vanished and her eyes flew open when he drew her into a close embrace, molding the softness of her curves to the hard lines of his body.

"Oh!" Selena gasped, then tried to recapture her smile. "Luke . . . isn't it?" she asked, silently cursing the sudden huskiness of her voice.

"Right." He didn't smile. "Branson," he reminded her. "We've met several times in the tour office."

"Yes, of course. I remember now." Selena worked at a casual tone. In truth, she was trying to forget those chance meetings in the offices. She hadn't wanted or appreciated the effect the sight of him had on her nervous system.

"Will you dance with me?"

Selena wasn't wild about the effect his low voice had on her, either. Squashing an urge to run for her life, she flashed her most brilliant smile at him. "Do I have a choice?" Since they were already moving in time with the music, she told herself the question was utterly ridiculous.

"Yes. Say the word and I'll walk away."

Like a coward, Selena longed to leap at the offer of escape, but she didn't. Dancing with him would be a test of her hard-won composure—a test that she fully expected to pass. Rising to her own challenge, she manufactured a light, careless laugh. "You needn't take a walk," she said with more confidence than she was feeling. "It's only a dance."

"Only a dance?" Luke smiled. "We'll see."

Selena didn't like either the sound of his remark, or his smile. Both did strange things to her equilibrium.

Her breath caught in her throat as he tightened his arms, drawing her into intimate contact with his taut body. Shock streaked through her as she was made aware of his state of arousal. Shock—and a frightening sense of excitement.

Caught, trapped within the confining circle of his arms and her own hardheaded pride, Selena automatically followed his lead. Her stomach churned when he placed one muscular leg between her thighs, and she was forced to clench her teeth to keep from crying out in protest against the flashfire his action ignited deep within her. Since her face was level with his chest, she had to tilt her head back to look at him.

"What do you think you're doing?" she demanded in a harsh whisper, silently damning the dark glasses concealing his eyes from her.

"Dancing?" Luke's soft voice held mocking laughter.

Selena snorted derisively and he laughed aloud. "I think you are being blatantly obvious," she said in a scathing tone. "And take those glasses off so I can see your eyes."

In one smooth motion, Luke raised one hand, whipped the sunglasses from his face, then replaced his hand exactly where it had been before... burning a hole in the sensitive skin at the base of her spine. "Is that better?"

"No." Selena managed a wry smile. "Better would be at least a foot of space between us."

"Not for me." Luke's eyes glittered in the semidarkness, making Selena sorry she'd demanded he remove the dark lenses. "For me, better would be closer." He enforced his statement by thrusting his hips into hers.

She gasped at the feeling of the power confined within the tautly-stretched jeans hugging his hips. Luke Branson was making his desire for her crystal clear. He was making her uneasy—and very angry.

Resentment shimmered through her and blazed like green fire from her eyes. "I'll ask you politely, one time, to back it up, Luke," she said in a fierce whisper.

"And if I don't, what will you do? Scream?" He arched his eyebrows and smiled with taunting arrogance.

"Oh, no. I wouldn't dream of raising my voice." Selena gave him an innocent look and a sugary smile. "But I wouldn't hesitate over raising my knee... forcefully." Her soft voice resembled the low purring sound of a feline. "Are you receiving my message?"

"Loud and clear," Luke muttered, withdrawing his intrusive thigh with extreme caution from between her legs.

Selena's expression turned wry. "I thought you might." With the heat of him removed, she resumed breathing and even managed a genuine smile. "Oh, dear, what a shame," she continued in a bright tone. "The music's ending and we didn't get our dance." He scowled. She laughed and slipped out of his arms. "Pity." Wiggling her fingers at him, she sauntered into the midst of the other dancers, out of harm's way.

Luke didn't appreciate feeling the fool...especially when the feeling was self-inflicted. His face hot, his mind cold, he walked to the edge of the patio and stared sightlessly at the river, running slow and sluggish from the extended drought.

Damned stupid ass, Luke raged at himself. Coming on to her like a sex-starved idiot was a dumb-kid thing to do. What had happened to his sense of subtlety?

Luke heaved a sigh of disgust and scowled at the placid river. He hadn't planned on making a pass at her—at least not this evening, and certainly not here in front of anybody who happened to be glancing their way. He had lost his legendary control, and that bothered him almost as much as looking the fool. Luke took particular pride in the fact that he never lost his cool.

But, damn, Selena did turn him on something fierce.

Across the width of the patio, Selena was chattering away like a magpie, laughing and even flirting a little with the blushing young man they all called The Kid. Inside, she was fighting a combined feeling of heightened excitement and raw panic that was too intense to tolerate.

Selena had put twelve feet of space between them, and Luke was still too close for her comfort. Her rebellious eyes insisted on slanting sideways glances at his tall, too-attractive frame draped lazily against the patio railing. The quick glimpses of the back of his neatly shaped head, the width of his shoulders, the narrowness of his waist, were enough to give her shivers. The sight of his trim, tight rear end and his long, muscular legs caused a dry pain in her throat.

It had been that way since the first time she had strolled into the tour office to find Luke similarly draped against the reception counter. He had had an effect on Selena she would not have believed possible prior to entering the office. His effect on her senses had intensified with each subsequent meeting. She didn't welcome the breathless, disoriented sensation he induced with his mere presence, and she didn't like it. But she didn't know quite what to do about it.

Selena's initial reaction had been self-protective in the emotional extreme. She had felt compelled to run as fast and as far as she could. But her sense of pride and cultivated self-discipline had come to her rescue. She would be damned if she'd run from *any* man.

Not that she had never run from a man. She had. Selena had retreated from several masculine advances. But that was before she had gathered herself and her defenses together, before she had formulated a set of rules—her own rules—to live by. And number one on her rule list was never again to allow any man to intimidate her in a sexual, or any other, manner.

The life rules had worked quite well for Selena for over five years. She had acquired the expertise necessary to maintain smooth working and social relationships with men. She had learned to laugh and tease and flirt and then adroitly dance away, unaffected and unscathed.

And then she had walked into the tour office and set eyes on Luke Branson. That one look had blown her rules and senses into shards of quivering, tormenting awareness.

Selena felt helpless, and she hated the feeling. Bristling with resentment, she slid another glance at him, just as he turned to stare directly at her.

In twilight, she couldn't see his eyes, but she could feel the impact of his stare. The shiver that feathered her arms, drawing bumps to the surface of her skin, had nothing to do with the gentle evening breeze. His silent observation unnerved her. His thoughts crept across the width of the patio to whisper to her subconscious. He wanted her, and he had every intention of having her. Selena felt it, knew it as surely as she knew the stark mountains in the distance would still be there with the next sunrise. The knowing scared the hell out of her.

Run, don't walk, to the nearest exit.

Selena obeyed the inner command without question, as she would a command to flee a burning building. As long as she remained in Luke's vicinity, she was in danger of being severely burned . . . from a different type of flame.

"Well, I'm going home. I've got an early float tomorrow morning." Selena made the announcement in a tone pitched to carry to the man lounging against the rail. She'd be drawn and quartered before she'd have him believe she was running from him . . . even though she was. "Anybody see my sandals?" She sent a frown around the patio, as if she didn't know what had become of her footgear . . . even though she did. She saw Luke turn and look down at the patio floor. Her breath caught as he shoved away from the rail. Bending, he scooped up her sandals and denim shoulder bag. Her heart thumped painfully as he ambled toward her.

"These what you're looking for?"

"Oh, yes." Selena forced a smile. "Thank you." She was careful not to brush his hands with her fingers as she took her things. "And good night," she added brightly—too brightly?—as she turned away.

"You're welcome."

Controlling the urge to dash away, Selena strolled toward the side of the house where everyone had parked their cars. Swinging her sandals in a carefree way, she called a general good-night to the others. Luke's voice was little more than a whisper, but she heard him, even over the light sound of her own voice and the thundering of her heartbeat. "Put your sandals on, you'll hurt your feet."

Pretending she hadn't heard, Selena kept moving. She let herself out through the gate in the patio rail and immediately stepped on a sharp stone. Muttering a curse, she gritted her teeth and forged ahead. She much preferred the pain in her feet, she thought, wincing as her tender sole pressed into another stone, than an injury to her emotions. Her body jerked when a low voice called to her.

"Selena."

She was about to dash the last few yards to her car when the voice called out again and she realized that the voice belonged to Brenda.

"Will you wait a minute? Where's the fire?"

Feeling ridiculous, Selena came to a stop. Working her stiff lips into a smile, she turned as Brenda caught up to her. "I'm sorry. I was thinking and didn't hear you."

"Must have been some heavy thoughts," Brenda said, panting. "Something worrying you?"

"No, of course not," Selena denied, thinking, not something, but *someone*. "What's up?"

The other woman gave a low, throaty laugh. "Well, we won't go into that. I just wanted to tell you not to be concerned if I'm not home when you get up tomorrow morning."

Selena arched her eyebrows. "Dave?"

"Yes," Brenda replied with blunt honesty. "He asked me to spend the night with him."

Selena was already concerned for her friend. Even as she told herself to mind her own business, she asked, "Is this wise, Brenda?"

The other woman shrugged. "Probably not, but you know I flipped for him the minute he showed up here out of the blue from Colorado."

"Hmm." Selena nodded. "But flipping and flopping are two altogether different things."

"Yeah, I know. Flipping brings on the urge for flopping." Brenda laughed. "Don't worry about me, Lena," she went on in a soft, serious tone. "I'm a big girl, in more than just my height. I can take care of myself."

"I know." Selena smiled. "But, all the same, I'd hate to see you get hurt."

"So would I." Brenda reached out to give Selena a quick hug. "Thanks for caring, friend, I appreciate it. But you know, you have to take a chance on being burned . . . if you want the fireworks."

Selena had never cared much for fireworks, considering them too dangerous to play around with. But she kept her opinion to herself. At thirty, Brenda was intelligent, mature and capable of making her own decisions, and the last thing she needed was pressure from her friend. Heeding her own advice, Selena backed away from the discussion.

"Then I guess I'll see you when I see you," she said.

"Right." Flashing a grin, Brenda turned back toward the patio. "Have a good night," she called over her shoulder, "and a good float tomorrow."

"Okay, thanks," Selena called back, watching as Brenda wove through the parked cars. She was about to turn again when she caught sight of a tall, dark form standing near the gate at the edge of the patio.

A tremor quaked through Selena's body. Her gaze fastened on the shadowed figure, as she slowly backed the rest of the way to her car. Her fingers shook as she inserted the key in the ignition. When the engine fired, she gunned it. The tires kicked up a spray of dust and stones as the car surged forward.

Seconds later, Selena glanced into the rearview mirror and her trembling fingers flexed, tightening into a death grip on the steering wheel.

Another vehicle had pulled onto the road behind her. Selena didn't need a roadside sign to tell her who the vehicle belonged to.

Luke was following her.

Why was he following her? Selena asked herself, gnawing on her bottom lip.

What did Luke Branson want of her?

Tension spiralled through Selena's body and she groaned aloud in protest. What did he want of her?

Dumb question.

Two

———

Luke had stepped from the lighted patio moments after Brenda slipped through the patio gate. He was reaching for the handle on the door of his dust-coated Jeep when he heard the engine of Selena's car turn over. He drove off the dirt lot adjacent to Will's house seconds after she tore away from the lot as though the devil himself was pursuing her.

Since the traffic consisted of just an occasional car or pickup truck, Luke had no difficulty maintaining a discreet distance while keeping her taillights in view. He brought the Jeep to a stop behind her in the dirt driveway leading to her house as the lights on her car flicked off.

Selena stepped from her low-slung, racy-looking car into the direct glare of the higher-placed headlights on his vehicle, and froze. Luke felt a strange twist of emotion deep inside at the look of her. Her eyes were wide, her expression startled, which was understandable. But what jolted Luke was the hint of fear visible in her starkly illuminated face.

Fear? The word stabbed into Luke's conscience. Selena had to know it was he...she must have seen him pull out behind her when she tore away from Will's place. And yet she looked cornered, poised for flight, like a doe ready to leap for cover.

Luke cursed himself in disgust as he stared into her still, light-washed face. Dammit! The last thing in the world he'd wanted to do was frighten her. His purpose was seduction... not intimidation.

They moved simultaneously, ending the moment that had seemingly frozen in the soft spring night. Luke pushed the door open and stepped out of the Jeep. Her eyes flashing green fire, Selena raised her chin as she turned fully to confront him.

"Why did you follow me?" Her voice was taut with suppressed anger and trepidation. "What do you want?"

You. The response leaped into Luke's mind. Choosing prudence, he left it there. "To talk," he answered in a soothing, even tone. "I only want to talk to you."

"About what?" she demanded, stepping back and watching him warily as he strolled toward her.

Luke raised his hands in a pacifying gesture. "About my boorish behavior at the party." Though the admission came hard for Luke, he was glad he'd

made it, for it drew an immediate, tension-easing reaction from Selena.

"At least you realize that you did behave badly,"
she said, wryly. "That's something...I suppose." She
shifted her gaze from him to his Jeep, arching her
eyebrows as she squinted into the glare from the
headlights. "You'd better talk fast. Those lights will
drain your battery."

Luke felt his lips twitch in amusement. "Not that
fast." He controlled the urge to smile when she slid her
cat eyes back to him. "I was hoping you'd be neighborly and invite me in for a drink."

"Were you?"

"Yes."

Broken only by natural night noises, the silence
stretched between them while Selena studied him
through narrowed eyes. It was obvious to Luke that
she didn't trust him. Barely breathing, he quashed his
gnawing impatience. His breath eased in a soundless
sigh from his tight chest when she gave a short nod of
acceptance.

"Okay, I'll be neighborly and give you a drink."
She flicked her hand at his car. "Switch the headlights off, then come into the house," she said,
abruptly swinging away. "I'll start a pot of coffee."

"Coffee?"

She didn't bother to glance back at him. "Coffee,"
she repeated in a definite tone.

"Whatever you say." Though Luke's voice con-
tained a sigh of regret, it was woven through with soft
laughter.

His laugh got to her. Or was it the repressed sigh? Shaking her head in despair, Selena unlocked her front door and entered the dark house. Leaving the door ajar, she flicked the wall switch, bathing the living room in a muted glow from the table and floor lamps. Dropping her shoulder bag onto the end of the curved couch, she kicked off her sandals and headed for the kitchen.

Was it his sigh or his laugh?

Selena considered the question as she stood at the sink, filling the glass pot from the cold water tap. Then again—did it really matter? What earthly difference did it make whether it had been the sound of his sigh or his laughter that had touched a chord inside her? Other than annoyance value, Luke Branson meant nothing to her, absolutely nothing. He wasn't friend or enemy. He was simply there.

Of course, that was the problem. He was there, and his being there unnerved Selena. The effect of his presence on her nervous system was brought home to her a moment later when suddenly, Luke was *there*, in her kitchen, standing within scenting distance behind her. He smelled delicious, a combined scent of pure male, healthy sweat and tangy bath soap.

Selena started.

Luke laughed.

Her question was answered.

It was definitely the sound of his laughter that got to her. The masculine, sexy sound of his laughter. Damn him.

Turning carefully to avoid touching him, Selena
drew on her composure to give him a chiding smile.
"You're crowding me, and I don't like it."

"Sorry." Luke took a half step back and smiled
when she frowned. "That's why I followed you home,
to apologize for crowding you at the party."

"Then why are you doing it again?" Selena arched
one winged eyebrow to add emphasis to her pointed
demand.

"Because you smell so damn good." Luke's casual
shrug underlined his blunt reply.

Uh-huh. Oh, boy. Yes, indeed. The pithy thoughts
tumbled through Selena's mind as she edged along the
countertop in a sideways move to escape. There was a
flutter inside her, a flutter unfamiliar, yet recogniz-
able. And, considering the fact that the flutter had
been caused by his casual compliment, Selena figured
she was in trouble, especially since she had just decided she liked the scent of him. Yep. No doubt about
it. She could very well be in deep trouble.

"Ah . . . coffee!" Whipping around, Selena pulled
open a cabinet door and thrust her hand inside. Cups
rattled. Soft laughter swirled around her, through her,
invading her mind and senses. It was heady. It was
dangerous. It was weakening. Selena fought the sensations with the only weapon available. Clutching two
cups, she slowly turned to glare at him.

"I amuse you?" Her voice was edged with ice.

"You arouse me." His was honeyed with warmth.

Selena's insides began to melt, instilling an exciting
mixture of panic and anticipation. She gulped, and
grasped for a straw.

"Is this your way of apologizing?" As straws went, it was a weak one, but it was all she could dredge up out of the sensuous haze clouding her ordinarily clear mind.

The tiny lines radiating from the corners of Luke's eyes crinkled with the hint of a smile that twitched at his lips. "For some reason, you have an extraordinary effect on my libido. Sorry." Luke shrugged again.

Selena felt the rippling motion of his shoulder muscles from her mind to the tingling soles of her bare feet.

Unfair! she protested in silent rebellion. It simply wasn't fair for any man to look so appealing, so handsome, so devilishly sexy by executing a casual shrug. It was unfair to the female population at large, and to her in particular. In desperation, she strove for the ultimate weapon of defense—her sense of humor.

"Strange," she murmured in a consoling tone. "But there seems to be an epidemic of weak libidos in the men out here in the wilds of West Texas."

Her gentle barb struck him smack on the funny bone. Luke gave a appreciative chuckle.

There was a subtle change taking place inside him. Something was different. Luke didn't relish the feeling, but he couldn't deny it. Selena was proving to be not at all as he had expected. Yet, in a way, she was, in fact, everything he had expected. The seeming contradiction confused Luke. It was a condition with which he was unfamiliar, thus decidedly uncomfortable.

He had to give this confusion some consideration. He had to think. Without conscious direction, Luke backed away, figuratively and literally.

"Coffee ready?"

She didn't hear him. More accurately, Selena didn't register the content of his question. She heard his voice. It had an odd, strained quality she couldn't quite define. But she wasn't listening too closely. She was caught in a web of bemusement, induced by the fluid movement of his tall, slender body.

Water.

The descriptive word surged into Selena's mind as she watched Luke back away from her.

Gently flowing water. Soothing. Comforting. Exciting.

Selena mentally frowned. Exciting? Could a physical action be both comforting and exciting?

The answer came in the leap of her pulse. Oh, yes. The two seemingly incompatible terms merged and blended in the lean form of Luke Branson when he moved.

It was downright demoralizing.

"Selena?"

"Huh?" She blinked.

"Coffee?"

A rush of flustered heat brought lucidity. Selena drew a quick breath and expelled a short burst of laughter. "Yes!" Idiot! she berated herself. Get it together! "I mean, of course the coffee's ready."

Selena was nothing if not efficient and quick. Her motions were economic and spare as she poured the coffee, collected sugar and milk, and set a plate of cookies, the chewy oatmeal she'd baked two days ago, on the table.

"Coffee is served," she announced, inviting him to the table with an elegant sweep of her arm.

The gesture set her gleaming black hair cascading around her shoulders and her breasts swayed gently. Luke swallowed to moisten the sudden dryness in his throat and groaned a silent protest against the delicious tightness in his body.

No question, the woman was a cat-witch, pure and simple. On second thought, Luke mused, easing his taut frame onto a slat-backed chair, there wasn't a thing simple about it, and forget pure. While seated on a solid wood chair, set on an equally solid tiled floor, he had the uncanny sensation of being inextricably mired in a bog of quicksand.

For Luke, who took pride in always being in control, the feeling was more than a little unsettling.

His fingers twitched from a reflexive urge to twine into the waist-long strands of her silky hair. His palm itched with a longing need to test the weight of her breasts. Luke wrapped his fingers around a cookie and filled his palm with the coffee cup, deriving little satisfaction from either of the tactile substitutes.

What was he thinking? Selena sipped at her hot drink and observed Luke surreptitiously over the rim of her cup. There was a strange expression on his handsome face, and he was staring at the cookie in his hand as if he'd never before seen anything quite like it. He looked hungry, but not for the chewy sweet he was contemplating.

He raised his eyes from the cookie. His gaze tangled with hers. His thoughts were revealed in the depths of his dark eyes, blatant with desire. A shiver performed the fandango down Selena's spine. She didn't need to hear the words spoken. She knew what he was thinking.

She was the selection of choice on Luke's personal dessert menu! In eloquent silence, he was informing her of his intention to have her served, not on a silver platter, but between the sheets of his choosing.

Selena swallowed, then swallowed again. It didn't help. Her throat was dust dry, parched, aching, throbbing in rhythm with an expanding ache deep inside of her. She gulped the coffee and shuddered as the hot liquid blazed a trail from her tongue to her stomach.

Luke's incredibly long eyelashes flickered as he lowered his smoldering gaze from her eyes to her throat, then to her moistened lips. His eyes devoured her mouth. The shiver dancing on her spinal column went into a frenzy. The throb inside her contracted into a tight ache of unspeakable longing.

He didn't utter as much as a murmur, yet Selena heard his impassioned cry as clearly as if Luke had shouted his needs and desires aloud.

She trembled.

His heated gaze monitored her tremors.

This was crazy! A tiny, sane portion of Selena's mind broke through her bemusement in outrage. She was immune to this sort of silent seduction, she reminded herself. She had gained that immunity through exposure to the shattering infection of mindless physical demands. Had she persevered and won her hard-fought victory over force, only to succumb to the power of a pair of glittering, devilish dark eyes?

"No!" The sharp sound of her own voice startled Selena as much as it did the man seated opposite her.

"No—what?" Luke blinked, frowned and then laughed. "I haven't asked you yet."

Oh, yes, you have! Selena bit back the retort. "Asked?" she said, repressing a shudder as she watched him sink his strong teeth into the cookie.

Luke chewed the sweet and washed it down with a deep swallow of coffee before responding to her hesitant query. "I was going to ask you if you'd mind if I came along for the ride tomorrow."

Selena went blank. "Tomorrow?"

Luke gave her an odd look. "Didn't I hear you say you have a half-day float tomorrow?"

"Oh, yes!" Selena smiled outwardly and groaned inwardly. "I mean, yes, I do have a float tomorrow."

Luke smiled and polished off his cookie. "The usual time... nine o'clock?"

"Yes." Selena frowned. "You want to come along?"

"If you wouldn't mind."

Mind? Of course, she'd mind. "No, of course, I wouldn't mind," she lied, with a strained smile. "I'm just curious as to why you'd want to go. Surely you've been on a half-day before?" Selena arched her eyebrows.

"Yes." Raising the cup, Luke drained its contents. There was no way he would admit to the curiosity about her expanding inside his mind, but he was de-

termined to observe her in her working environment.
"But I haven't been on a float with the accepted expert guide," he explained in a deceptively offhand
tone of voice.

Did she detect a slight dig there? Selena mused. A
mild slur against her status of expert? Positive that
Luke was being chauvinistically condescending, she
bristled. Feeling both insulted and challenged, she
flashed her most brilliant counterfeit smile.

"It's only a half-day float and the river's low. It's
not going to be very exciting, but—" she shrugged
"—I have no objections to having you along." In
truth, Selena had not only objections, but serious reservations about being the target of his observation.

"Good." Luke set his cup on the table and slid back
his chair. "Thanks for the coffee." He stood and offered her a derisive smile. "And I do apologize for
earlier."

Right.

Selena swallowed the uncharitable thought while
responding, politely, "Apology accepted."

"And now you'd like me to leave."

She inclined her head. "It is getting late."

Luke shot a glance at his watch. "All of ten-
fifteen." He laughed, but turned to go. "I'll be at the
warehouse early to help with the equipment."

While she heard him with a part of her mind, another part was busy fighting the melting effect of his
soft laughter, and her voice sounded vague. "Okay.
Thank you." She swallowed. It didn't help. She swallowed once more. "Good night."

"Good night." Luke nodded, took a step back, paused, then, moving with blurring, silent swiftness, circled the table to loom over her. "It's not going to be a good night," he muttered, bending to her. "It's going to be a lousy night."

His last words were murmured close to her mouth. Selena felt his moist breath on her lips, caught the scent of coffee with her senses. "Luke..."

He drank her protest with his hungry mouth. His lips were cool and firm, not passive, but not demanding, either. The pressure his mouth applied to hers was minimal, yet Selena felt the resultant ripples in every nerve ending she possessed. The sensation was shattering. She wanted more. But before she could respond, the pressure was removed. Luke straightened and moved back, away from her. She stared up at him in frustrated confusion.

"Take that good-night with you to your empty bed," he muttered. An instant later, the front door closed with a soft click behind him.

Luke was gone, but the vibrations of his presence hummed in the still air, drumming against Selena's senses. Unmoving, she sat staring at the empty kitchen archway, absorbing the echoes of all the words that hadn't been spoken between them.

What was it about this man? she mused, shivering in response to the cool breeze wafting through the open kitchen window. At least, she told herself that her shiver was in reaction to the night air. Oh, without doubt, Luke Branson was the most masculinely handsome man she had ever had the misfortune to come in contact with. But, she reminded herself, she had never been impressed with mere good looks or the attraction of a long, muscled male form. And she had certainly never been impressed by a cool kiss!

So why was she feeling so very hot inside? What was it about this particular man? His personality? Selena made a grunting noise. Not likely. Since he had proved himself to be both aggressive and irascible, overlaid with arrogance, Luke's personality left a lot to be desired.

And yet, something about him, inside him, had spoken in silken whispers to something inside her.

The memory of the effect, the continuing effect, of those whispers, strengthened by the tantalizing taste of his brief kiss, intensified the shiver playing havoc with Selena's nervous system. A low moan slipped through her lips, startling her from her reverie. Scraping back her chair, she jumped up and began to gather the coffee things together.

"Sheer chemistry." Selena spoke aloud, in a harsh tone aimed at dispelling Luke's lingering vibrations. "That old black magic. The siren song of hormones." The table cleared, she headed for her bedroom. Pausing with her hand on he light switch inside the smooth plaster archway, she ran a jaundiced glance around the room. "Ah, the mystery of it all." She grimaced and rolled her eyes. "Ha! Baloney!" She hit the switch, plunging the room into darkness.

But Luke's prediction proved stronger than Selena's bravado—it was a long, lousy night.

The next day started out bad and went downhill from there. After a restless, dream-strewn night, Selena awoke with a nightmare of a headache.

It was all Luke's fault, she grumbled irritably to herself, wincing as she tugged a brush through her sleep-tangled hair. Why did he have to come to this particular part of Texas, anyway? The thought stilled her fingers in the act of plaiting three thick sections of her hair into a single braid.

Where had Luke come from? And why? Selena frowned at her reflection in the dresser mirror. She was aware that all of Will's employees were dropouts of one type or another—including Will himself. Selena knew them, recognized them, because she was one of them. But there was something different about Luke. The difference was subtle, hard to define, but it was there.

And it bothered her.

Impatient with him and with herself, Selena flipped the long braid over her shoulder and, slanting a wry look at her scowling image, turned away from the mirror. It was getting late. She didn't have time for reflections—of any sort. She had a job to do.

The day was warm and pleasant. The river was placid. The paying customers were congenial. The work would have been a pleasure for Selena if it hadn't been for one member of the group. Even though, in all reluctant honesty, she had to admit that Luke had kept his promise by arriving early to help her and the two recently hired trainee river guides who were working the float with her.

Had he been almost any other man, Selena would have appreciated his assistance. Quite like her, Luke worked efficiently. He loaded the equipment at the supply warehouse and then unloaded it again at the launching spot on the river in less than half the time required by many others she could name.

But why did he have to look so darned good? Selena asked herself at regular intervals while greeting the tourists, and again while chatting with them during the short bus ride upriver, and then while instructing the group on the hows and whys of their life jackets.

And why did he look so good to her? she chided herself, steadying the raft while Luke gallantly assisted the ladies in the party.

His attire—cutoff jeans, a T-shirt, rubber-soled sandals and a straw hat—was similar to that worn by most of the other guides, herself included. Yet somehow, on Luke's slim, muscular body, the clothes took on a certain elegance.

But was it the clothing or the man?

Avoiding the dangerous question, Selena leaned on the long oar to push the raft away from the sandy shore and into the river's slow current.

There were three rafts for the half-day trip—two small, one large. Selena had taken the lead in the larger raft. The other two rafts, each carrying four customers, trailed at a safe distance behind her. In her raft was a party of eight—three middle-aged couples, herself, and Luke.

The three women were seated on the seat in the front of the raft, exclaiming over every bird, turtle and even domestic animal they spotted. Their husbands and Luke were perched on the inflated sides and back of the raft. Selena was happy to be in the guide's position at the center of the craft. With the necessity of facing forward to steer, Selena didn't have to look at him.

She was earning her salary, Luke observed, while absently listening to the conversation among the men on either side of him.

In fact, Selena was working up a healthy sweat.

He gave the appearance of being utterly relaxed, with his long legs stretched out in front of him and his feet crossed at his ankles. But Luke was alert to every nuance of the woman standing before him.

Concealed by dark sunglasses, Luke's narrowed eyes focused on Selena's slender form. Beneath her smooth, tanned skin, her feminine muscles rippled as she plied the oars to keep the raft moving in the sluggish current. The late-morning sunrays poured over her, sheening her skin with a fine film of perspiration.

Luke wet his lips and fought a sudden intense desire to glide the tip of his tongue down the enticing hollow of her spine. In that instant, he wanted her so badly his hands trembled. He wanted to test the strength she was applying to the oars, experience her supple motion as she wrapped herself around him. He wanted to feel the slickness of her aroused body sliding against the passion-drawn wetness of his.

"Hot, isn't it?"

Hotter than hell. Luke held his tongue and gave a wry smile to the man seated on his left. "Yeah," he replied. "And it's only mid-April. They tell me that I'll be gasping from the heat by early June."

"You're not a native?"

"No." Luke shook his head. "I'm originally from Pennsylvania, outside Philadelphia."

"Could've fooled me," murmured the man, who had introduced himself simply as Chet, a C.P.A. from Maine. "I'm glad we decided to take our vacation in the spring this year, instead of summer."

"Your first time in West Texas?" Luke asked, trying to sound interested, while fighting a silent battle of control with his clenching body.

Chet nodded. "First time in the Southwest, actually." He nodded again to indicate the slightly overweight woman seated on the right side of the raft. "Texas was my wife's idea." His expression turned droll. "She suggested it right after she finished reading a book about the Alamo."

Luke grinned. "Have you been to San Antonio?"

"Yes. Beautiful city. We all loved the River Walk."

"Oh, then the six of you are traveling together?" Luke asked, skimming a glance at the other five members of the group.

"We're related," Chet said, laughing. "Besides that, we get along fine. We've been vacationing together for the last five or six years now."

"I see," Luke murmured, certain that what he saw were three couples who no longer felt a need for romance or the privacy necessary to indulge that need.

For some reason, the idea bothered Luke. He was relieved when one of the women excitedly drew his attention to something moving in the water.

"Yes, it's a snake," Selena said, using the oars to slow the raft's motion. She called back to the other two guides to draw their attention to the reptile, then leaned forward to peer at it. "It could be a bull... I can't tell for sure at this distance."

"Are there a lot of snakes around here?" Chet's wife asked, staring at the riverbank with a new intensity.

"Oh, they're around," Selena replied. "But, you know, snakes are really shy creatures. They avoid confrontation rather than look for it. Why, I've been on the river for four years now and I've only seen three or four snakes in all that time."

"And on land?" the woman persisted.

"I've seen a few," Selena admitted. "But only rarely where there's human traffic." Her smile was reassuring. "They're not like some animals, human or otherwise. They don't come begging for handouts."

"But the cashier at the general store told my husband that there was a snake right outside his trailer just yesterday morning," the woman seated in the middle of the trio piped in, shuddering visibly. "He said it was a rattler and that he almost stepped on it."

Selena angled her head to slant an amused look at Luke before responding to the woman. "And did your husband offer the cashier his other leg?"

"What?" The woman looked blank.

The four men at the rear of the raft chuckled.

"The cashier," Selena said. "That was Jasper Chance, and I believe he was pulling your husband's leg... just a little. Jasper likes to add local color for the tourists so they don't go away disappointed."

"Oh!" The woman laughed in appreciation. "Then if we're careful, we have nothing to be anxious about . . . I mean, when we stop for the snack that's included in the float?''

"Not a thing," Selena said reassuringly. "As all of you will realize in a few minutes," she continued, steering the raft toward a gently sloping section of the riverbank, "this is where we're stopping for the promised snack." Her eyes danced with humor as she swept a glance over the group. "And, if any one of you spot a snake, please don't hesitate to bring it to my attention." Her lips curved in a delightful smile. "Because I want to see it, too."

Her smile went straight to Luke's senses.

Three

Bemused, confused and rattled, Luke sat in the sketchy shade cast by a scraggly tree and picked at the food he'd absently placed on his paper plate.

As snacks went, the one provided by the tour agency was lavish. Working competently together, Selena, the other two guides and Luke had set out an array of finger food fit for the best restaurants anywhere.

In addition to a shrimp dip, which Selena whipped together, there was a selection of cheeses, pickles, olives and crackers. There were thick slices of summer sausage and smoked oysters. There were nuts, potato chips and pretzels. And for dessert, there was an assortment of cookies, plus slices of fresh apples and oranges.

Luke sampled everything . . . and tasted nothing.

He was more than distracted. His thoughts were fractured, skimming off toward middle-aged couples vacationing together one second, then bouncing along a different path to rest on the emerging and surprising facets of Selena's character.

He gave only token attention when one of the tourists exclaimed over what he thought was a goat. The creature was perched precariously on the side of the steep bluff that loomed over the arroyo where the group had made temporary camp. Luke did notice, and was impressed by, Selena's response.

Busily slicing more oranges for the hungry group, she glanced around and up, narrowed her eyes, and pronounced, "It's not a goat, it's a horse." She immediately returned her attention to the job at hand.

The skeptical tourist was inclined to argue. "Nah, that can't be a horse," he insisted, craning his neck for a better look. "It must be a goat."

Since Selena didn't answer, but merely shrugged, Luke decided to settle the question. Setting his plate aside, he got up and ambled to where he'd stashed his backpack with the tour supplies. Retrieving his binoculars from the pack, he adjusted them and zoomed in on the animal.

"It's a horse," he said, offering the glasses to the other man so he could see for himself. His expression still skeptical, the man took the glasses and raised them to his eyes.

"Damned if it isn't!" He lowered the glasses and gave Selena a sheepish smile. "You were right, miss."

Selena responded with a flashing smile and a quipped, "I get paid for being right."

Groaning silently in protest against the effect her smile had on his central nervous system, Luke collected his plate of barely touched food. He dropped it into the large trash bag clipped to the side of the folding table beneath the only shade tree in the arroyo.

Although he deplored the waste of food, Luke knew there was no way he could force another morsel past the odd tightness in his throat. Annoyed with himself and with the new and puzzling emotions he was experiencing, he turned to one of the large water coolers that had been fastened at the front of each raft. Ignoring the containers of instant tea and lemonade mix provided, he tapped a paper cup of clear spring water.

The cool liquid slid down his throat, easing the dryness, but having no effect on the closed, clenched feeling. Impatience riding his nerves, Luke walked away from the group. Striding along the arroyo bed, he walked until he could no longer hear the muted sound of their voices.

The silence was pervasive, soothing, thought provoking. Soaking the sunlight and the quiet into his skin, Luke pondered his own sense of disquiet and tried to sort through the thoughts converging into a jumbled heap inside his head.

Staring at the rugged landscape without really seeing it, he centered his mind on the strangeness of his feelings. For the life of him, Luke couldn't recall a time when he had felt so uncertain, so disoriented about his own emotions—not even in his early twenties, when he met his ex-wife.

For as long as he could remember, Luke had always had his life and head together. He was certain of what he wanted and knew exactly how to go about achieving his personal and professional goals. Even in the devastating wake of divorce and the British court's denying him any custodial rights to his little girl, Luke had had no doubts about how to proceed.

He had literally thrown himself into his work, producing masterpieces of architectural design that had won him worldwide acclaim. And, along with the fame, he had suddenly found himself the object of feminine attention—very willing attention. Still riddled with bitterness, and so without a hint of compunction, Luke had availed himself of all the delicious, ego-soothing favors offered by the lovely females.

But that was before a small dynamo of a green-eyed woman had breezed into the tour office and his life, messing up his mind and emotions.

The very idea of being uncertain was enough to give him indigestion. Luke absently raised a hand to massage the dull pain gathering in his temple.

Dammit! he fumed. Why was he doing all this internal agonizing? He needed a woman and had set his sights on Selena. Why was he complicating the issue? Selena was just another woman, no better, no worse. And, in all truth, considering the tormenting hell his body was giving him, it would be to his advantage if she *were* worse than any other woman—at least, in a moral sense.

Sharp pain streaked through Luke's head. Closing his eyes, he applied deeper pressure to his throbbing temple with massaging fingers.

"Luke."

Because it was the one voice he wanted most to hear, he thought at first that it came from the hidden, lonely area inside his head.

"Luke, where are you?" Selena called out in a very real, impatient tone. "It's time to go."

"I'm here," Luke replied, sighing. He lifted his hand from his temple to settle the straw hat more firmly on his sweat-beaded brow. "I'm ready."

"Well, for heaven's sake, what have you been doing back here?" Selena asked, spotting him as she rounded the bend of the arroyo. "Or is that an indelicate question?" Her grin was both impish and rakish.

"I've been communing with nature," Luke drawled. And myself, he added silently, striding toward her.

"Are you all right?" Selena peered at him from beneath the brim of her own smaller hat.

Luke scowled. "Of course, I'm all right. Let's go." He moved to walk around her, but she stopped him in his tracks by grasping his arm, revealing a surprising strength.

"Luke, wait! Are you sure?" Her frown was fierce. "You look odd, pale, too hot."

He was too hot, inside and out, but not from the merciless rays of the sun. He was on fire, burning with desire to be with her, inside of her. He needed her, the silkiness of her, the heat of her, her passion—not, by damn, her compassion.

Jerking his arm free of her grasp, Luke glared at her. "Yes, I'm sure. I'm fine." He scowled. "You want proof?" Without plan or design, he reached for her. Grasping her upper arms, he pulled her to him, tormenting himself by molding her soft curves to the hard angles of his overheated body.

This time there was no reserve, no lack of emotional impact to his kiss. Luke's mouth didn't merely touch Selena's parched lips, it devoured them. His mouth was hard, hot, hungry. In an instant, she was drowning in a cauldron of moist heat. Her mouth was on fire, her senses were ablaze, her emotions inflamed. She felt the tip of his tongue flick her closed lips, seeking, then demanding, entrance. Helpless to do little else, she opened her mouth to allow him passage. The results of her instinctive reaction were devastating.

Luke's tongue surged into the wet sweetness of her lemonade-flavored mouth. Then, as if incited by the sweet-tart taste of her, he groaned and plunged his tongue to the depths, searing the delicate tissues with his urgent spear of possession.

In that brief moment of union, Selena was his and she knew it. He could do as he wished with her—exert his will, draw her to the ground and take her, there and then, in the ruthless rays of broad sunlight, and she would not, could not, have stopped him—in truth, she would have helped him.

Fortunately for Selena, Luke either didn't realize—or chose not to take advantage of—her weakened position. Cursing under his breath, he released his grip on her mouth and arms. Then, shaking his head, he drew away from her with a muttered, "Let's get back to the others."

Her body made taut by her internal battle to absorb the tremors quaking through her, Selena stared in numb bemusement at the demoralizing attraction of Luke's retreating form. What had she said to earn for herself both the literal and figurative sharp edge of his tongue? In an absent, reflective move, she skimmed her tongue over her lips, gathering the lingering sting of his bruising, arousing kiss. All she had done was ask if he was feeling all right and touched his arm. What was so wrong in that?

Men! Shaking her head, Selena struck out after him. Would she ever understand the male of the species? A wry smile quirked her lips. On the other hand, did she really want to understand them, especially the deep, dark-souled ones like Luke?

Shrugging off the unusual and unwanted excitement his kiss had induced within her and the strange concern she was feeling for him, Selena trudged along the arroyo until she caught up to the group waiting for her.

"We're off," she announced, avoiding the tall, silent man standing beside the larger raft. "And I do mean in more ways than one." Tossing an encouraging grin at the two trainee guides, she leaped into the raft.

Luke spent most of the remainder of the float time in a brown study. He was angry—at himself, for his abrupt and physically torturing response to Selena's concern for his welfare—and with Selena, for her initially impersonal attitude. And yet, even in his brooding state of distraction, he couldn't help but notice the expert way she handled the ungainly raft while keeping an eye on the two inexperienced young men trailing at a safe distance behind her.

Oh, yes, Luke conceded, Selena was very good at what she did. He experienced a memory of her heated response to his kiss and was forced to stifle a reflexive groan. He wanted more of her, a lot more. He ached to test the depths and breadth of her talents. Her multifaceted expertise was evident on several levels, even on this slow, seemingly interminable half-day float.

The tourists lost some of their enthusiasm as the morning gave way to early afternoon. Like hothouse flowers, they began to wilt from exposure to the glaring sunlight. Still, they were game when Selena, still wearing her life jacket, slipped over the side into the water, inviting any and all to join her.

To Luke's amazement the women followed Selena fully clothed, taking time only to kick off their sandals. Though the men opted to remain in the raft, they called encouragement to their wives, and laughed good-naturedly when the ladies gave them a soaking by dousing them with water.

"This feels great," Chet's wife said, splashing happily. "You ought to try it."

"No, thanks," Chet replied dryly, pulling his damp shirt away from his chest. "I'm about as wet as I care to be."

Drawn out of his moody reverie, Luke arched his eyebrows and smiled wryly. "Do they always literally throw themselves into their vacation activities like this?" He inclined his head to indicate the laughing, bantering females.

"Pretty much so," Chet replied sardonically. "But, then, they pretty much throw themselves into any and all the activities they get involved with year round. As my wife, Carol, says, 'This is the only shot we're going to get at this life, so we may as well wring as much enjoyment as possible from it.' And the rest of us agree with her."

"That's as good a life philosophy as any others I've heard," Luke murmured.

"That's the way we figure it," one of the other men, named Norm, chimed in. "And, to our way of thinking, it sure beats suffering in silence."

The unintended shot hit home for Luke, with his accumulated years of bitterness and anger. Wounded, but determined not to revel his pain to anyone, especially strangers, he dredged up a smile and a shrug. "Whatever works," he said, dropping the subject.

The float continued without incident after the women scrambled back into the raft, sodden but happy. Luke sighed with relief when they finally arrived at the landing site a few miles from the tour office.

The bus was waiting for them, parked under a large tree near the bank of the river. Selena was also relieved to see the trip end, if only for the opportunity to part company with a certain too-attractive and too-disturbing member of the party. Luke Branson unnerved her, undermined her self-confidence, and Selena took pride in never allowing herself to be unnerved or undermined by any man.

With the combined efforts of Selena, Luke, the two guide trainees and a couple of the male tourists, the rafts and gear were quickly stowed onto the trailer attached to the bus. Selena was about to slip behind the wheel of the vehicle when she was gently but firmly moved aside.

"You navigated the river," Luke said before she had a chance to protest. "I'll drive."

Without protest, Selena slipped onto the seat directly behind him and almost immediately wished she hadn't. Due to the peculiar position of the bus, Luke had to practically manhandle the oversized vehicle as he backed it around to face the rutted dirt road leading away from the river.

The effort he was forced to exert brought every one of his back, arm and shoulder muscles into play. Selena was fascinated by the smooth coordination of the thews and tendons beneath his sun-browned skin. The bus was air-conditioned, yet she began to perspire as her imagination took flight.

Inside her mind, images formed of Luke's hard mouth lavishing her soft lips, of his long, lean body gliding sensuously along the length of hers. The brief fantasy was so real, Selena thought she could actually feel his tongue glide into her mouth, his muscles and tendons contracting in reaction to the intensity of his passion.

A burst of laughter from one of the men behind her brought Selena to her senses. She never fantasized about men! Shocked and embarrassed by the wayward wanderings of her mind, she sat up straight and firmly turned her gaze toward the window. Selena couldn't recall ever feeling so glad to see the tour office as she was when Luke finally brought the lumbering vehicle to a halt before it.

Then there was the confusion of everybody leaving the bus, with handshakes, thanks for a great time and shared laughter over the three women's wet clothing. Finally, goodbyes were exchanged as the tourists went their separate ways. Giving a last wave, Selena turned to get back on the bus. There was still gear to be unloaded at the warehouse. The two younger guides were on the bus, and Luke was already behind the steering wheel. She had leaped onto the first step when Will shouted to them from the office doorway.

"Hey! Hold up a minute."

Poking her head out the open door, Selena asked, "What's up, Will? Trouble?"

"Hell, no." Will laughed. "At least, I hope not. After you guys unload, go home and get on your fancy duds. I'll expect you at the restaurant by seven for the big celebration."

"What are we celebrating?" Selena asked with a smile, knowing full well that Will never needed a reason for a party.

"An engagement," Will said, grinning back at her. "Brenda told me this morning that she and Dave are going to bite the bullet and get married."

"Married!" Selena gaped at him in sheer astonishment. "Are you serious?"

"I am." Will nodded. "And, from all indications, so are Brenda and Dave."

"What they are, is seriously crazy."

The unsolicited opinion came in a dry voice from the man seated behind the steering wheel.

Though Selena agreed with Luke in principle, she resented his presumption and his tone of voice. Brenda was her friend, Selena fumed. And as a friend, *she* was allowed to consider Brenda's decision precipitous and foolhardy. But Luke was an outsider and had no right to pass judgment. Narrowing her eyes, Selena slowly turned to pin him with a glittering stare.

"Brenda and Dave just might be in love," she said in a lowered voice that held dangerous overtones.

"Sure," Luke drawled, meeting her glare with cool detachment. "And those ancient mountains just might disappear by tomorrow morning." He jerked his head to indicate the rugged spires of the Big Bend.

Anger flared through Selena and flashed from her green eyes, yet she managed an icy tone. "Can I assume from your attitude that you will not be attending the celebration?"

"You may assume anything you like," Luke retorted. "But I wouldn't miss the party for the world."

Selena bared her teeth in a feral smile. "Too bad," she muttered, swinging up onto the second step of the bus. "I was looking forward to having a good time." Presenting her back to him, she strode to a seat midway back. Luke's soft, taunting laughter stalked her every step of the way.

Both the sound of his laughter and the word *married* haunted Selena.

In a state of mild shock induced by the news of her friend's sudden decision, Selena was able to ignore the welter of emotions Luke's presence created inside her throughout the time required to unload the float gear. And she escaped to her car as soon as the job was completed.

Selena had hoped to find Brenda at the house when she arrived home. She wasn't there, but proof of her recent occupancy littered the place from the living room to Brenda's bedroom. Thinking that unless her friend got her act together, she'd make a lousy home-maker, Selena collected the articles strewn from one end of the small house to the other.

Homemaker. Selena shook her head in despair as the word echoed in her mind. Try as she would, Selena could no more imagine Brenda as a wife and homemaker than she could herself in the domestic role. The image just didn't fit, somehow.

Hot and tired, Selena flopped onto her bed to contemplate the unbelievable reality of the coming nuptials. Brenda of the glib wit and fierce independence—married? Impossible. Selena was very much afraid that her friend had succumbed to the effects of a mind-numbing night of fantastic sex.

Selena grimaced and smothered a yawn with a languid hand. She would have to talk with Brenda, she decided, giving in to the weight tugging on her eyelids. They needed to have a long, private, woman-to-woman, straight-from-the shoulder talk. The decision made, she sighed and drifted off to sleep.

* * *

The restaurant and adjacent bar were packed when Selena arrived a little before eight o'clock. Music blared from Will's prized antique jukebox. Squashed together on the small dance floor, couples gyrated to the rock-and-roll beat. And yet, in that crush of bodies, the first person Selena spotted was Luke.

He was standing at the bar—rather, he was lazily draped against the bar, as he had been on the patio rail at Will's house and against the counter in the tour office. And, exactly as it had before, the sight of him sent tingles of awareness and anticipation scurrying throughout her body.

Selena resented the sensation and resented him for causing it. Irritated, she swept a disdainful glance over his lean form, from the tip of his boots to the neatly brushed, gleaming hair on his head.

Luke was dressed much like most of the men in the place, in casual slacks and short-sleeved sport shirt. But the attire was where the similarity ended. The other men appeared nice and presentable. Luke was sexy and devastating. And he was looking intently at Selena.

Had she parked her broom outside the door? The whimsical thought wandered through Luke's mind as he stared at the woman poised inside the entrance. The sight of her turned his insides to molten liquid.

She was wearing a sundress patterned in splashes of lilac and green on a white background. The full skirt swirled around her slender legs, and the snug-fitting bodice accentuated her enticing breasts. Her bare shoulders gleamed in the glow of the muted light.

Her hair was loose again tonight. Freed from the braid the black waves cascaded over her shoulders and down her neck. A yearning to coil his fingers in those silky strands and curl them around his body, binding his naked form to hers, engulfed him, making his throat dry and his insides ache.

Selena.

Her name whispered through him, around him. Selena of the lithe body and cat-witch eyes and hair. His body reacted in the usual manner. Luke was glad he was propped against the bar, afraid that if he wasn't, he'd double over. He wanted her. The wanting blazed from his eyes.

His compelling dark eyes conjured erotic images both shocking and alluring. Without conscious thought, Selena took a step toward Luke, mindlessly obeying his silent summons. Commanded by the force of his will, she might have walked straight into his arms, if a familiar voice hadn't called to her, breaking the strange spell that mesmerized her mind and senses.

"Selena!" Brenda shouted over the din of mingled voices. Selena saw that she, Dave, Will and a group of others were seated at a large table at the edge of the dance floor.

Smiling and returning calls of greetings from friends as she went, Selena wove her way through the crowd. She gave Brenda a quick hug when she finally reached the table, then deliberately turned the chair they had saved for her so that her back was to the bar. The large table could comfortably seat ten people, and there was only one other empty chair—the one next to Selena. Absently wondering who they were saving the last chair for, she managed to produce a bright smile.

"I hear congratulations are in order," she said, shifting her glance from Brenda to Dave.

Dave had a silly grin on his face and Brenda looked ecstatic. "Yes," they answered in unison.

"Isn't it romantic and exciting?" the young woman seated next to Will asked in a bubbly, enthusiastic tone.

Selena slid her gaze to the pretty woman. Her name was Marilyn Trent. She was an experienced river guide and had been working for Will for about eight months. Since Selena had been away for six of those months, she didn't know Marilyn very well. But she had heard since her return that Marilyn was friendly, outgoing and popular with the locals as well as the tourists. Marilyn was also known for her tender heart—and less-than-virtuous behavior. Figuring the woman's personal life was her own business, Selena liked her, although she didn't agree with her opinion in this instance. However, she certainly had no intention of throwing a damper on the festivities by voicing her concerns. But some clearly did not share her reservations.

"Romantic and exciting, Marilyn?" Luke spoke in a cool tone from behind Selena, startling her. "I'd say it was more impetuous and prosaic."

There was a moment of stunned silence, during which everyone except Selena stared in astonishment at Luke. Then Brenda eased the sudden tension with a burst of laughter.

"Oh, Luke, you're such a grinding wet blanket," she said chidingly. "Why don't you just keep your gloom-and-doom thoughts to yourself, sit down and pass out the drinks?"

It was as he moved around her and closer to the table that Selena noticed the large tray Luke was holding. It was laden with glasses, some filled with wine and some empty, and two pitchers of beer. After setting the tray in the center of the table, he settled himself in the chair next to her.

Even as she stifled a groan of protest against his proximity, Selena was forced to admit to herself that, of all of them, Luke had been the only one with the courage—or gall—to give voice to his true opinion of Brenda and Dave's impulsive decision to get married. Conversely, knowing it was none of Luke's or anybody else's business, she silently endorsed Brenda's advice that he keep his opinion to himself.

"Dance?"

Luke's voice was close, too close, and pitched low, yet it jolted through Selena like an unexpected shout. While her mind rebelled at the idea of being held once again in his arms, her body quivered with anticipation. Cursing her physical reaction to him in silent frustration, she turned her head to stare at him with cool disdain. "After being treated to your style of dancing last night?" she asked, arching her eyebrows. "I don't think so."

Luke had the grace to at least appear repentant, but his eyes gleamed with devilment, proving that appearances were often deceiving. "Would you reconsider if I promise to be very, very good?"

Selena had no doubt that Luke could be exceptionally good, indeed. It was exactly what he was good at that bothered her. Her raised eyebrows took on a skeptical curve. "There'll be no clutching or overt moves?"

While his dark eyes continued to taunt, his expression grew somber. "You have my word."

"Uh-huh," she drawled, not trusting him for an instant. But, while she harbored mental reservations, her body decided the issue by propelling her to her feet. "Okay, I'll take you at your word," she said, since she seemed to have little choice in the matter. "But I'm giving you fair warning," she continued, allowing him to lead her onto the floor. "Make one move out of line and you'll be dancing by yourself."

Luke's only response was a muscle-clenching, mind-bending rumble of soft laughter. Bemoaning the unfairness of any man possessing a laugh that sexy and appealing, Selena moved with extreme trepidation into his waiting arms.

As it turned out, Selena's fears were groundless. Luke was the soul of propriety throughout the series of slow romantic songs someone had selected on the jukebox. Perversely, she felt a confusing sense of disappointment when he escorted her back to their table.

Luke did not ask her to dance again. Instead, he spent the rest of the evening dancing and flirting with Marilyn—in a manner Selena considered both obvious and outrageous. Not surprisingly, the other woman reveled in his attention, and clung to his lean body while on the dance floor—and to his every word while off it.

Determined to ignore the sight of Luke and Marilyn laughing together, along with the unsettling pangs it was causing deep insider her, Selena concentrated on enjoying the party. She danced with Dave, Will, Jasper Chance and even The Kid. She talked and laughed. She even managed a few minutes in private with Brenda when they went to the ladies' room, although their conversation was brief and mainly concerned Brenda's future sleeping arrangements.

"I'm staying with Dave," Brenda said when Selena asked if she'd be coming back to the house that night. "But I'll still pay my share of the rent for the month."

"I'm not worried about the money," Selena said, dismissing the idea with a shrug.

Brenda smiled and gave her an impulsive hug. "You've been a good friend, Lena, and I don't want you worrying about me, either."

"Because I'm your friend, I can't help but worry," Selena murmured, returning the hug.

"Well, don't," Brenda said briskly, stepping back. "Will it be okay if I come over tomorrow to collect my junk?"

Selena laughed. "Of course. I'll even help you, since I'll be free for three whole days."

"Are you going to lecture me?" Brenda demanded, grinning impishly.

"Discuss," Selena replied, grinning back at her.

"Well, in that case, no problem." Brenda's grin wobbled. "Will you stand beside me at my wedding, Selena?"

"I thought you'd never ask," Selena said, grasping Brenda's hand. "And, if you hadn't, you would have been in trouble. Of course I'll be beside you, you nit."

Arm in arm, laughing together, they returned to the celebration.

To her annoyance, the first thing Selena noticed was that Luke was once again on the dance floor with Marilyn, his head lowered over hers, as if in intimate conversation.

"I'm sorry, Marilyn, I couldn't hear you over the music." Cursing himself for his lack of attention, as well as the other woman who was causing his distraction, Luke gazed down into the sparkling blue eyes raised to his—and wished they were green. "What did you say?"

"I asked you what you're thinking about." Marilyn's tone and smile were at once conspiratorial and suggestive. "Or can I guess?" she said, moving her hips into alignment with his as she trailed her fingers up his spine.

Luke had to control an urge to stiffen under her too-familiar touch. "I'm thinking that this situation is getting too hot too soon." He forced a languid smile when he felt her fingers brush his collar. "I wouldn't want to be accused of rushing you into anything."

"Oh, rush me, rush me." Marilyn's voice was little more than a breathless murmur.

Luke barely heard her. From the corner of his eye, he caught Selena's movement as she headed for the door. Cursing to himself, he dragged his attention back to the eager woman rubbing against him. "No." Though he infused a rueful note into his tone, his voice was adamant. "You've had too much to drink and I can't allow myself to take advantage."

Marilyn muttered something, but this time, Luke didn't hear her at all. Turning her in rhythm with the slow music, he watched in narrow-eyed frustration as Selena made her way toward the door to slip away from the party—and him.

The pangs pulsing inside Selena intensified to a definite ache when she saw Marilyn slide her fingers up the back of Luke's neck and into his hair.

She didn't care what they did, of course, Selena told herself, dragging her narrowed green eyes away from the couple. It was just that their display was so blatant, so damned obvious in intent. There probably wasn't any question in anybody's mind where Marilyn would be spending *her* night!

Blaming her disgruntled feelings on the blaring music and the raucous talk and laughter, Selena called a general good-night to her companions and headed for the door, adroitly skirting the dance floor, where Luke and Marilyn were plastered together, moving as one to the evocative music.

Although she was disgusted with herself for doing it, Selena kept glancing into the rearview mirror throughout the drive from the restaurant to her house. The road behind her remained dark, free of two high-set headlights.

Four

It was late—or early, depending on one's point of view. Except for the occasional trailing wisps of clouds, the night was clear, the spring breeze refreshing and cool. The glow from millions of stars and a three-quarter moon illuminated the landscape, casting the rugged mountainous terrain into sharp relief of light and shadows. It was a night for poets…or lovers.

Pacing the length of the patio of the house he was renting from Will, Luke was too sensitive, too attuned to the sensuous allure of the soft night.

Luke was neither poet nor lover. The absence of the former talent didn't bother him. The abstinence imposed by the privation of the latter was the reason he was awake, restless and prowling the patio.

His body was tight, and he felt too large for his taut skin. The ache deep inside him was more intense and unnerving than a sore, throbbing tooth. He craved release, yet had denied himself the satiation his body demanded by rejecting the opportunity when it had been offered to him.

Throughout the course of the evening, Marilyn had made it clear, without actually saying it aloud, that she would be more than willing to spend the night with him. But, although he had deliberately centered the majority of his attention on the eager young woman, Luke had left the party alone, less than a half hour after Selena had gone.

What had he hoped to prove, anyway, by playing up to Marilyn? Luke grimaced and retraced his pacing steps across the patio. He didn't have to delve too deeply into his motives to come up with the answer to his question. He had been trying to prove his own adage, which was that any woman would do if the need was great enough.

The fact that he was alone and hurting merely underlined the utter failure of his exercise. Even now, hours later, Luke could hardly believe that he had not taken advantage of Marilyn's willingness. He needed a woman. The need was a living torment to his mind and body. A week ago, twenty-four hours ago, he probably wouldn't have hesitated in accepting her invitation, since it had been issued with obvious, if silent, honesty and with no strings attached.

Luke knew himself. He was a sensuous man by nature. He loved making love. His nature had cause the initial rift in the early days of their marriage, because his wife was the exact opposite. She found the sexual side of marriage too earthy and was not averse to voicing her opinion, often and disparagingly.

Of course, Luke had known almost at once that the marriage was in trouble—he was living in a near-constant state of frustration, so he couldn't help but know. What had amazed him was the realization that he hadn't discerned his wife's true character, even though she had played the part of eager partner before the legal knot was tied.

But, if he was sensuous by nature, Luke was also moral, ethical and loyal. He would not have as much as contemplated alleviating his frustration with any woman other than his wife.

But Selena wasn't his wife.

The startling thought brought Luke's pacing to a dead stop. Scowling, he stared into the darkness beyond the wall enclosing the patio. He was doing it again! In reliving the frustration he had suffered at his former wife's coolness, Luke realized that he was denying himself satisfaction in exactly the same manner as he had during the cold, empty years of his marriage.

The mere idea was preposterous, Luke thought, shaking his head in negation of the concept. Why would he inflict torment on himself out of a sense of loyalty to a woman he hardly knew? It was more than preposterous, it was absolutely nuts.

Selena McInnes was a stunning woman. Luke knew his initial reaction to her beauty was as natural as breathing. He was a healthy man and like most healthy men, his body responded of its own volition to a beautiful, sexy-looking woman. It was as simple and physical as that. But beyond that immediate response, there had been, and continued to be, an undeniable and strong attraction between them. Luke felt it, and intuitively knew that Selena felt it, too.

His sense of loyalty didn't come into play, he assured himself, resuming his measured paces.

Then why had he rejected Marilyn's offer?

The unwelcome and unpalatable question stabbed at Luke's mind and again brought his restless motion to a halt.

At that very moment, he could have been reveling in the bounty of Marilyn's lush curves, or savoring the sweet exhaustion of afterglow. He could be rested and satisfied, rather than prowling his patio like some wild animal.

Selena.

Dammit! That black-haired, green-eyed woman was the reason he couldn't rest. Selena and her mindbending, on-again-off-again, don't-get-too-close attitude. After her startling, exciting response to him in the arroyo, Luke was convinced that, deny it though she may, Selena felt the same strong attraction to him. And yet she persisted in keeping him at arm's length—which was exactly why he had deliberately given his attention to Marilyn.

But his ploy hadn't worked. Though Luke genuinely liked Marilyn, his body hadn't responded to hers, not even while in the most intimate embrace while they were dancing.

Yet the mere thought of Selena set his pulse pounding and his body on fire.

Damn the woman for having the power to turn off his natural inclinations and screw up his thinking.

Disgusted with himself and his own mind-abrading thoughts, Luke made a growl deep in his tight throat. The feral sound was absorbed by the predawn silence.

It was quiet, too quiet. Angry, aching, restless, Luke glared into the darkness in defiance of a creeping, inner sensation that he was the only living being in the world.

Would the night ever end?

Cradling a mug of coffee in her palms, Selena stood at the wide window in her dark bedroom, staring into a more complete darkness beyond the pane. Behind her, her bed had a rumpled, deserted look. Inside, Selena *felt* rumpled.

She yearned for sleep. Her eyes felt gritty, her eyelids heavy and puffy. Yet sleep had eluded every method of inducement she had employed.

Selena self-righteously placed the blame for her nocturnal disquiet at the feet of the handsome, tormenting devil masquerading as Luke Branson.

She had tried counting sheep, only to find a two-horned wolf laughing at her.

She had tried the premeditation exercise of relaxing her muscles from the feet upward. But instead of being enfolded within a blanket of relaxation, she was a prisoner of the image of a tall, dark-eyed seducer.

Exhaling a deep, tired sigh, Selena sipped at the cooling brew, then grimaced as the tepid liquid burned its way from her throat to her stomach.

Indigestion. It happened every time she drank cup after cup of coffee, especially at night. Selena shuddered and made a face of distaste at the sour, burning sensation in her chest and throat. Her soft lips growing tight with determination, she turned away from the window.

Her hinges must be loose and her gate swinging free, she decided, striding out of the bedroom. She needed sleep, not the added agitation of coffee-induced heartburn. She glanced at the clock as she swept into the small kitchen.

Five past three. Selena groaned and marched to the sink. It wasn't fair, she railed in silent protest, dumping the contents of her cup and the coffee remaining in the pot down the drain. It just wasn't fair that Luke had the singular power to rattle her mind like this, keeping her sleepless and aroused.

Aroused?

Selena stiffened and became still, appearing frozen in place at the sink.

Aroused? She repeated the word in silent, fearful wonder. Aroused? Selena probed her emotions for an answer. It came, swift and blunt. Yes, dammit, she was physically, sensuously aroused, and had been since she had walked into the tour office two weeks ago to find Luke lounging against the counter. Selena didn't like the sensation of acute physical awareness.

A tremor snaked down her spine. She was never turned on by a man—any man. In fact, until now, she had believed herself immune to the erotic attractions of the opposite sex. Yet, here she was, sleepless and trembling at the mere consideration of a particular male of the species.

Uneasy, her breath constricted, Selena spun away from the sink and rushed into her bedroom. Her thoughts pursued her, stabbing with unrelenting persistence into her mind.

She wanted Luke Branson. She was longing to experience the thrill and excitement of feeling her mouth and her body crushed beneath his. She was burning with a sudden, raging need to have his strength fill the emptiness inside her.

But this wasn't possible! The silent protest screamed inside Selena's head. She had been cured of sensuous attraction to men, not once but on three separate occasions. Her memories of those humiliating encounters didn't bear thinking about.

In a bid to deny the flood of remembrance, Selena tore off the oversize T-shirt she used as a nightgown. Feeling frantic, she pulled on a smaller T-shirt, shorts and her sandals. Scooping her handbag from the floor, she ran from the room, and then the house. She heard, but ignored, the shattering, shrill sound of her ringing phone.

Fortunately, the roads were deserted. Clutching the wheel of her sleek sports car, Selena tore through the early-morning darkness as if she were being pursued by the very devil himself—which, in a sense, she was.

But even driving at a speed exceeding the legal limit, Selena could not outrun her churning thoughts. Memories, sharp and clear, unraveled inside her mind, mingling with the taunting image of a man too masculinely handsome for anyone's good—especially hers.

Selena didn't want to remember, dreaded the very idea of those buried scenes. They infuriated and sickened her, but they were preferable to the new and frightening sensations the vision of Luke Branson created inside of her.

Selena was fourteen, naive and too trusting, when she received her first lesson on the perfidy of men. The man was in his late thirties and had been a friend and neighbor of her family for over ten years. He and Selena's father played golf together nearly every weekend. His wife and Selena's mother were close companions. Being childless, the couple had been granted the honorary title of "aunt" and "uncle" to Selena and her sister and two brothers.

And so, Selena was unwary and unaware of danger on the hot summer afternoon when her friendly neighbor just happened to drop in when she was alone in the house. Within minutes of his arrival, her honorary uncle was more than friendly—he seemed to be all hands, and every one of them was touching Selena in a shocking and intimate manner.

Momentarily stunned by his advance, Selena had endured his rough caresses. Then panic exploded inside her, clearing her mind when he forced her down onto the kitchen floor. Weeping, mindless with fear, she fought him like a wild thing in an effort to free herself. Her struggles only served to inflame him, increasing his determination. Muttering words of assurance that all he wanted was to teach her about what could be shared by a man and woman, the man clamped his mouth over hers. Holding her still with one hand, he then began tearing at her clothing with the other.

Selena's stomach churned when she felt his hand clutch at her bared breast. She was teetering on the edge of panic-induced unconsciousness when she was saved by the sound of her young brother's tearful voice.

"Mom! Where are you? I'm hurt!"

Her brother had been injured playing sandlot ball. His broken finger saved Selena's virginity.

Even now, fourteen years later, she felt a bewildering amazement at the memory of the swiftness of her neighbor's retreat. Within the few minutes required for her brother to search her out in the kitchen, her uncle had set her on her feet, straightened her clothing and dashed for the back door. Before escaping, he had snarled a warning against telling anyone about what had happened between them. She never did, not even after he and his wife moved away from the neighborhood a few months later.

Selena shuddered as the memory receded, then groaned in protest as another formed to take its place.

It was July, she was eighteen and excited about being the maid of honor at her older sister's wedding. Since Selena had been asked to stay overtime in the store where she was working for the summer, her future brother-in law had offered to pick her up and get her to the church for the wedding rehearsal.

Selena had liked and trusted her sister's future husband. He had quickly robbed her of both misplaced feelings.

Innocently chattering away about the forthcoming ceremony, she had not questioned the deserted route he had taken, until he pulled the car off the narrow road and parked beneath the low, concealing branches of a willow tree. Feeling her throat close from a flaring sense of unease, Selena had to force herself to look at him.

"Why have you stopped?" Selena heard the fear in her voice, and knew he heard it, too.

"Because you are too beautiful to resist," he answered, reaching for her.

It was a nightmare for Selena, a replay of the ugliness she had endured at the hands of her neighbor. But this time she was saved by a passing farmer, who stopped his battered pickup truck, thinking they were having mechanical difficulties. And, like her neighbor before him, her sister's groom warned her about saying anything to anyone, smugly claiming she wouldn't be believed if she did, since her sister was obviously head-over-heels in love with him. Suspecting the truth of his claim, Selena had remained silent.

The marriage had lasted less than a year. Selena's sister divorced her husband for his numerous infidelities.

Driving through the pitch-black night, Selena heaved a sigh of regret for her sister's unhappiness, then released the bitter memory, making room for yet another.

* * *

It was late August and Selena had recently returned to campus for her senior year of college. Though still a virgin, she was no longer innocent or trustful, which made the encounter with her roommate's boyfriend all the more humiliating.

He was the quarterback of the football team. He was tall, lean and boyishly handsome. Selena's friend was madly in love with him. Having learned her lesson the hard way about what she believed was the true nature of men, Selena was cynical but tolerant. In that state of mind, she had reluctantly agreed to meet with him when he'd requested her assistance in choosing a special gift for her friend.

It was only after the debacle that Selena realized that she should have followed her cynical bent and bagged the tendency toward tolerance.

The athletic hero made advances, revealing a penchant for physical domination.

"You know you want it," he had the unmitigated gall to say while attempting to force her thighs apart. "I'm good," he had boasted. "Just relax and I'll show you how much fun we can have."

Older and aeons wiser, Selena did relax—just long enough to position her right leg between his thighs. A moment later, he doubled over, bellowing in pain. Selena scrambled to her feet and walked away from the whimpering "hero," satisfied that it would be a while before he offered to show another unwary woman how much fun he could bestow upon her.

* * *

A traffic light, flickering from green to amber to red, caught Selena's attention. She slammed on the brake, bringing the car to a rocking halt at the intersection.

Intersection!

Selena blinked. Where in the world of Texas was she? Collecting her scattered wits, she glanced around. Her startled gaze came to rest on a highway marker.

Alpine! Selena frowned. She had driven close to a hundred miles and didn't remember a minute of it! Wondering what time it was, she glanced to the east. The first blush of pink stained the horizon.

The traffic light flicked again, from red to green. Still frowning, Selena set the car in motion and eased at a sedate speed through the intersection. Staying within the posted twenty-five-mile limit, she circled the block, intending to return home. She was approaching the intersection again when weariness struck her a staggering blow. Shoulders slumping, she headed the car in the direction of a familiar motel.

The night clerk was an acquaintance of Selena's. He gave her a room without hesitation or question. Clutching the room key, she mumbled her thanks, then made a beeline for the ground-floor room.

The room was clean and cool. Selena barely noticed. Not bothering to undress, she dropped onto the bed. Her last thoughts before sleep claimed her were of the tall, handsome man her body craved.

Her defenses undermined, Selena sighed and accepted the desire she was feeling for what it was. She wanted Luke Branson, wanted his caress, his mouth, his body.

Damn the devil.

The woman was driving him crazy.

The thought inciting action, Luke slammed the telephone receiver onto the cradle. Where in hell was she? He had rung her number at least ten times since somewhere around three-thirty that morning, each time hoping to hear the maddening sound of Selena's voice. It was now almost seven o'clock, and the only sound he'd heard was the ringing at the other end of the line.

Where was she? Who was she with?

Frustrated, angry and generally at his wits' end, Luke resumed his night-into-morning pacing.

Who was she with?

Luke came to an abrupt halt, his eyes narrowing as he examined the thought. The possibilities were endless. In addition to the regulars in and around the area, there was a constant turnover of male tourists in varying ages, shapes and sizes, unattached and unspoken for.

Luke scowled as he suddenly recalled one particular tourist. The young, attractive man had been with the tour group the day before, though assigned to one of the other rafts. In retrospect, Luke remembered that the young man hadn't seemed too happy about his raft placement.

Had the man approached Selena either before or after the party last night? Luke mused. Further, had Selena gone off with him after she left the party?

Could that have been her reason for slipping away so early?

More than half convinced his deductions were correct, Luke tormented himself by carrying them to what he considered to be their natural conclusion.

If Selena had met with the young tourist after leaving the party, had she then spent the night with him?

Images flashed into Luke's mind, explicit and erotic images of Selena, naked and vulnerable, in another man's bed. His muscles clenched around a queasy sensation invading his stomach as the images expanded against his will, filling him with green sickness and red rage.

"No!" Luke was unaware of crying the denial aloud, but he was painfully aware of the punishment he inflicted on his knuckles by ramming his fist into the adobe wall. "Dammit! Dammit!" he swore in a soft, lethal voice. "She is mine."

The sound of his own voice, the content of his muttered words, brought him to stillness. His? Luke frowned. The possessiveness in the concept startled him.

He wanted to possess Selena, yes, but . . . *his*, as in exclusively?

The answer came swift and positive from deep within his consciousness. Yes . . . his, as in exclusively, selectively, completely. . . . If any man was going to have Selena naked and vulnerable in his bed, that man had damned well better be Luke Branson.

Glaring at the phone as he passed it, Luke strode into his bedroom. Selena would have to come home sometime, and when she did . . . Cursing aloud, he flung himself onto the bed. He was dead to the world within seconds.

A burst of feminine laughter right outside her window startled Selena from a restless sleep. Confused, disoriented and wondering where she was, she glanced sleepily around the room. Memory returned as she absorbed her surroundings.

Pushing herself up on one elbow, she peered at the digital clock in the TV. It said 9:26. Since the edge of the drapes were rimmed with sunlight, Selena had to assume it was 9:26 in the morning, which meant that she had slept a grand total of four hours.

Selena didn't feel rested—in fact, she felt lousy. Delving into the unsavory encounters of her past had left a bad taste in her mouth. Deciding she needed about nine more hours of sleep, she eased back onto the bed. She was drifting off when another memory flashed into her head.

Brenda! She had told Brenda she would help her pack this morning! Scrambling up, she sat on the edge of the bed, lifted the phone receiver and punched in her home number. Brenda answered on the third ring.

"Selena!" Brenda exclaimed. "I've been worrying myself sick ever since I got here. Where are you?"

"In . . . Alpine," Selena answered reluctantly.

"Alpine! What are you doing in Alpine?" Brenda asked in a tone of amazement, then added, "Or is that an indiscreet question?"

"No," Selena said, smiling wryly. "I didn't have a secret rendezvous or anything like that. I couldn't sleep and decided to take a drive," she explained.

"When I got to Alpine, I felt too tired to drive back, so I checked into a motel."

"Oh."

Brenda's blank response brought a smile to Selena's lips. "I'm sorry I wasn't there when you arrived at the house," she apologized.

"Not to worry," Brenda said. "I've already collected all my assorted stuff and junk. Dave will be here to pick me up in a while."

"Well, in that case—" Selena paused, then thinking fast, continued "—I think I'll drive into San Antonio and do some shopping. A friend of mine is getting married, you know, and I want to buy a special dress for the occasion."

Brenda laughed. "Nothing too fancy," she cautioned. "Dave and I both prefer a simple affair."

"Okay, you're the bride." Selena shrugged. "Oh, and by the way, I'll probably be staying at the motel on the river, in case you or Will should want to reach me."

"Good luck," Brenda drawled. "Or had you forgotten this is the week of Fiesta?"

Selena groaned aloud. She had forgotten. "Oh, well, I'll just have to take my chances. If you don't hear from me, that's where I'll be. If I can't get a room, I'll call you after I get there and let you know where I'm staying."

A simple affair. The phrase ran through Selena's mind repeatedly as she tooled along Route 10 a few hours later. There wasn't a simple thing about the idea, in her opinion. Marriage to any man had to be the most difficult thing imaginable.

But then, marriage and an affair were two altogether different things, weren't they? she mused, fighting a persistent image of a tall, handsome devil of a man.

They were, Selena assured herself. Marriage demanded total commitment, while all that was required in an affair was the commitment of one's body. And, after ruthlessly examining her feelings throughout every mile traversed between Alpine and San Antonio, she was almost, but not quite, prepared to commit her body to an affair.

Selena still wanted Luke Branson. It was as simple—and scary—as that. But wanting him and bringing herself to the point of indulging were two entirely different things. She was scared and running, and she knew it. Which was the reason she had decided to give herself some breathing space by going to San Antonio.

Five

"San Antonio?" Luke frowned. "What's she doing in San Antonio?"

"The Mexican hat dance," Brenda shot back in a breezy, mind-your-own-business tone. "Who wants to know, anyway?"

Luke didn't know Brenda very well, but he knew her well enough to realize that flippant though she might be, she wouldn't tell him anything unless he identified himself. "It's Luke Branson, Brenda," he said, struggling to control his tone. After only three hours of sleep, Luke was not the most patient of men.

"Oh. Hi, Luke, what's up?" Brenda's voice was still breezy, but the suspicious edge was gone. Before he could respond, she asked, "Is Will looking for Selena?"

"No. At least, not as far as I know," he added truthfully. "I'm not in the tour office, I'm at home." Catching sight of his hand, Luke scowled and loosened the stranglehold his fingers had on the telephone cord. "I . . . er, just called to ask Selena something," he explained, improvising, since he wasn't about to tell Brenda that the "something" had to do with his bed—and the lady in question.

"Well, as I said, she's not here," Brenda said. "And I won't be, either, in a few minutes. Sorry."

Not as sorry as I am. Luke didn't voice the disgruntled thought. Instead, afraid she was about to hang up, he said, "When did she leave? I mean, it's not noon yet, and she was at the party last night."

"Yeah, I know." Brenda laughed. "She must have taken off soon after she left the party. She told me she spent the night in a motel in Alpine."

With who? Luke bit back the question and a searing expletive. His narrow gaze scored his rumpled bed. Dammit! From all indications, it seemed that while he'd been sweating out the long hours of the night, Selena had probably been laughing and partying in a motel room some distance away. "And now she's in San Antonio?" Luke asked in a pleasant tone that he pushed through his gritted teeth.

"I doubt she's there yet!" Brenda laughed. "I know Selena drives fast, but she doesn't drive that fast! I expect she'll get there around dinnertime."

Unless she and whoever she's with stop along the way. Luke again kept the thought inside his head, and blandly said, "I see. Okay. Thanks, Brenda."

"You bet," she replied. He was about to hang up when he heard her call, "Oh, Luke!"

"Yeah?"

"Tell Will that if he wants to reach Selena, she'll probably be at the motel on the river."

"Probably?" he asked.

"Yes, probably," Brenda answered. "She said she was going to give the place a try, even though it is Fiesta Week."

Luke frowned. "Fiesta Week?"

"Sure, you know," she said. "Fiesta San Antonio? It's a yearly event in Texas. It draws thousands of tourists from all over the country."

Although Luke did recall reading something in the paper about the Fiesta, he had forgotten the dates. "Big time, huh?"

"Party time," Brenda said on a laugh. "There's lots of entertainment and great food. You ought to check it out while you're here in Texas."

Luke's smile was grim. "I just might do that," he said, knowing there was no "might" about it. "Thanks again, Brenda, I'll talk to you later."

"Right. Bye now."

After depressing the disconnect button, Luke punched the number for the tour office. Will answered on the first ring.

"It's me, Will," Luke said. "I won't be able to help out in the office for a few days. I have some personal business I have to take care of."

"What are you trying to do, Branson, bring me out of retirement?" Will asked in a mock growl.

Luke's set expression was softened by a smile. Will was the least retired retiree Luke had ever run across. "A little work will do you good," he retorted. "You don't want to get too lazy and comfortable, do you?"

"Very funny," Will grunted. "Any idea how long you'll need to complete your business?"

"A couple days, give or take," Luke said with deliberate ambiguity.

"Okay, I'll look for you when I see you."

"Right," Luke said, then added, "By the way, I spoke to Brenda and she asked me to tell you that Selena is in San Antonio, probably at the motel on the River."

"San Antonio?" Will repeated. "What in hell is she doing in San Antonio?"

"Beats me," Luke drawled. "I only agreed to relay the message."

"Well, damn, she's only back from South America two weeks," Will grumbled. "Women! Who can figure 'em?"

"Not me. See you, Will."

A shower, shave and change of clothes later, Luke was behind the wheel of the Jeep, driving at a speed guaranteed to add yet another layer of dust to the vehicle.

"You're in luck, Ms McInnes." The attractive desk clerk's teeth flashed startling white in contrast to his dark skin. "Since we just received word that some of our guests have been delayed and will be unable to keep their reservation for tonight, there is one room available."

"But only for the one night?" Selena asked, swallowing a sigh of weariness.

"Yes, I'm sorry." The clerk's mouth curved into an encouraging smile. "But something might turn up tomorrow."

Selena couldn't resist returning his smile. "All right, I'll take it. I'd be a fool not to."

The clerk gave a sage nod. "Fiesta Week," he murmured, sliding a card across the desk to her. "If you will, fill out this registration card, please?"

"Yes, of course." Selena peered at the identification tag on the young man's lapel. "Thank you, Mr. Montegra."

"Manny, please." The young man made the request in a soft, coaxing voice.

Selena arched her eyebrows in surprise. "Manny?"

His teeth flashed again. "Yes, Manny. It's short for Manuel."

His grin was so infectious, Selena found herself grinning back at him. "Okay," she agreed. "Manny it is."

"Gracias."

"You're welcome." Her lips still twitching with amusement, Selena concentrated on filling out the registration form. When she'd finished, she slid the form and her credit card to him.

With obvious and flattering reluctance, Manny turned away to take an imprint of her card. "Thank you," she said when he returned.

"My pleasure." Manny sounded as if he meant it. His soft dark eyes did a swift but comprehensive ap-

praisal of her face and body, lingering briefly on her
unconfined breasts beneath her thin T-shirt.

Selena felt a jolt of awareness, not of Manny, but
awareness of her attire and appearance. "Ah...would
you happen to know how late the shops are open?"
she asked, determining to buy herself a change of
clothing.

"During Fiesta?" He shrugged. "Most establish-
ments remain open quite late." He handed the room
key to her. "If I can serve you in any way, please don't
hesitate to call on me."

Whoa! Selena thought, as she turned away from the
desk. Talk about service with a smile!

She parked her car in the attached parking deck and
made her way to her room on the sixth floor. There,
she caught a reflection of herself in the dresser mirror.

No wonder Manny had given her so much attention, Selena thought, appalled at the sight of herself.
She looked beat, which she was, but beyond the signs
of weariness, she looked like a... The word that
sprang to mind didn't bear thinking about. Tossed
around by the wind whipping through the open windows of her car, her hair was a tangled black mass
tumbling down her back. The brief amount of sleep
had left her eyes shadowed, almost sultry. Worst of all
the perspiration dewing her body had molded her shirt
to her torso, revealing the gentle curves and high tilt of
her breasts.

She needed a shower, and she needed some sleep.
But first and foremost, Selena told herself, she needed
to splash cold water on her face, brush her hair and go

shopping. Ten minutes later, she shot a longing glance at the bed, heaved a heartfelt sigh, then strode from the room.

Dangling the idea of sleep in her mind like a motivating carrot, Selena went through the first boutique she came to like a whirlwind. When she emerged less than an hour later, her arms were weighted by packages and her wallet was a lot lighter.

She made a quick stop in a drug store for toiletries before returning to her room in the motel. Dumping her purchases onto a chair, Selena stripped and stepped beneath a soothing hot shower spray. Then, her shampooed hair still dripping and her body naked as a newborn, she put in a wake-up call for eight-thirty, slid between the sheets, sighed with relief and was asleep within seconds.

Except to fill the gas tank and grab a cup of coffee, Luke didn't stop. He made it to San Antonio by nine o'clock that night. And, by the time he pulled into the curved, covered driveway in front of the motel, he wasn't sure which he was more hungry for... Selena, sleep or a thick steak.

His body provided the answer the instant he stepped into the motel lobby. Every muscle Luke possessed tensed as he caught sight of Selena. Her glorious hair cascaded to her waist in loose curls and waves. She was dressed in an off-the-shoulder peasant blouse and a full, brightly patterned skirt. Large gold hoops adorned her ears and heeled sandals displayed her calves to advantage. From where he stood, Luke could see the sparkle in her emerald-green eyes. She was standing at the reception desk, smiling up at a tall, slim young man.

Luke didn't recognize the man, but that didn't matter. He disliked him on sight. Positive he was looking at the man who had spent the night with Selena in Alpine, Luke narrowed his eyes, curled his fingers into his palms, and coolly sauntered to the desk.

"Hello, Selena." Though Luke's voice was low, she reacted to it as if he had shouted her name. Her head swirled in his direction, sending her hair flying around her shoulders. At any other time, he might have found her expression intriguing.

"Luke!" Selena exclaimed in a startled gasp. "What are you doing here?"

Exerting a measure of control over an urgent desire to shoulder her companion aside, then pull her into his arms, Luke forced his fingers to relax and hooked his thumbs into the back pockets of his jeans. "Do you mean here, in this hotel?" he asked in a languid tone. "Or here, in San Antonio?"

"Both," Selena replied, shifting her glance as if looking for someone—or an escape route. "This is the last place I would have expected to see you."

"Really? Why?" Luke arched his eyebrows and looked bored. Inside, he felt ready to explode.

"Why?" Selena gave him a blank stare. "You work for Will. I mean, if you're not there, who's draped over the counter at the tour office?"

"Draped over the counter?" Luke repeated, losing a battle against a grin.

Selena fought and lost a battle of her own, and though her smile was faint, it lit up the dark places in Luke's soul. "You know what I mean," she said in a chiding tone. "You're lounging against the counter every time I come into the office."

"Yeah, well..." he began, only to be interrupted by the soft voice from the young man Luke was so pointedly ignoring.

"If you will pardon me?"

"You rang?" Luke slid him a glittering look that provoked a visible shudder.

"Er...*señor*?" Manuel wet his lips.

"Yes?" Luke bared his teeth in a wolfish grin.

Selena exhaled a harsh sigh of exasperation. "Luke, this is Manuel Montegra." Her scowl changed into a smile as she turned to the other man. "Manny, meet Luke Branson."

"A pleasure, Mr. Branson," Manny murmured politely, extending his hand.

"Yeah," Luke grunted, unhooking his right thumb to clasp the hand in a brief shake.

"You'll have to forgive Mr. Branson his bad manners, Manny," Selena said impatiently. "It seems that he's been in the hinterlands too long." She leveled a quelling look at Luke before again offering a soft smile to Manny. "What did you want to say?"

Manny's slim, elegant face showed definite signs of confusion and strain. "I only wished to excuse myself," he explained, warily edging away from Luke. "I have an appointment and it is getting late."

"Don't let me detain you...*señor*."

"Luke, please!" Selena shot him a quick look of pleading exasperation. "Then you must leave, of course," she said to the baffled clerk. "Thank you for everything, Manny."

What *everything*? Luke felt prickles of unease stab his imagination. What had Manny done, what service had he supplied, to warrant Selena's warm thanks? Luke slid his left thumb from his pocket and flexed his fingers. Manny's shirt was open at the collar, revealing a smooth, slender throat. Startled, Luke realized exactly what he was contemplating.

Was he losing his mind? More to the point, was he allowing his desire for this woman to scramble his brain?

Disgusted with himself, Luke forced his taut muscles to relax, and he even managed a cool smile as Manny turned and walked away.

"Would you care to tell me what you were trying to prove by being so unpleasant?"

Luke's smile warmed up as he switched his now-undivided attention to Selena. "Was I unpleasant?"

Selena made a face. "You were very rude." Her expression changed from annoyed to confounded. "Why?"

Since Luke wasn't about to admit to himself that he was bristling with jealousy, he certainly wasn't going to admit it to her. Instead, he pulled a long face. "I'm sorry. I haven't eaten all day."

Selena was skeptical, but she chose not to pursue the issue beyond a slight dig. "Well, I haven't eaten much today, either, but it hasn't made me rude."

"I said I'm sorry." Luke's serrated tone gave clear warning that he wouldn't apologize again.

Selena shrugged and offered him an arch look in response. "I heard you."

A slow grin tugged at his mouth. "Good. Now, since I have your attention, and since we're both hungry, why don't you let me buy you dinner?"

"So you can be rude to me?"

The grin teasing his lips did a flying leap into his dark eyes. "Selena," he said in a shivery purr. "Believe me, the last thing I want to do is be rude to you."

Selena gave him a considering stare. "I'm not at all sure I like the sound of that."

Luke gave a tension-relieving laugh, then said, "My intentions are good. I'm offering to buy you the biggest steak dinner we can find before I collapse from starvation. Will you join me?"

She hesitated, then gave in with a gracious smile. "Yes, thank you."

Luke had to draw a careful breath before he could speak. "Okay." He exhaled. "But, first, hang loose. I've gotta see if I can get a room for the night."

"You don't have a reservation?"

He shook his head as he stepped up to the desk. "No. Keep your fingers crossed." He swiftly learned that it wouldn't have helped if she'd crossed not only her fingers, but her toes, arms and legs, as well. The desk clerk was polite, but there simply wasn't a room available.

"No luck?" Selena asked as he turned, frowning, away from the desk.

"No." He shook his head.

"Fiesta Week," she explained.

"Yeah," he shrugged. "I don't know San Antonio at all. Can you suggest another place?"

Her expression wasn't encouraging. "Yes, but I really doubt you'll have better luck at any one of them."

"Right." He sighed. "Damn, I'm hungry."

Selena stared at him, gnawing on her lower lip, then, as if coming to a sudden, difficult decision, said in a rush, "I'll share my room with you."

Luke wasn't surprised at her offer—he was stunned into absolute stillness. "What did you say?" he asked after his rejoicing senses settled down.

From the look on her face, it was evident that she was reconsidering. "Of course, if you'd rather not..." She shrugged as her voice trailed away.

Rather not? Luke would rather not have eaten for a month before dreaming of turning her offer down. "Green Eyes, I may be rude on occasion, but I'm never stupid," he said. "I'd be both grateful and honored to share your room."

"Yes, but will you be good?" she asked with unintentional provocation.

Luke's smile was a study in advanced sensuality. "I'll be more than good," he promised in a tingle-producing murmur. "I'll be terrific."

"We-ll . . ."

"What room are you in?" Luke inserted, before she could change her mind. "I'd like to clean up a bit before going out to dinner."

"I only have the room for tonight."

"You're driving back tomorrow?" Luke frowned.

"Unless I can find another room." Selena shrugged. "But at this moment, the prospects look slim."

"Yeah, well, at this moment, I'm too hungry to worry about it. What room are you in?" he repeated, pointedly.

Selena rummaged through her bag. "It's self parking here," she said, handing her room key to him with noticeable reluctance. "I'll wait back there for you." She indicated a seating area toward the rear of the lobby. "There's a side exit onto the River Walk from there."

"Fine." Luke took the key firm in hand. "I'll make it as quick as possible." Controlling an urge to leap into the air and let out a loud victory whoop, he smiled and sauntered to the door.

Luke was gone about twenty minutes. They were the longest—and shortest—minutes of Selena's life, as she agonized over the prudence of her hasty decision.

Though it was true she had accepted the idea of Luke as her lover, Selena wasn't at all certain she was prepared to encounter him quite so soon.

Second thoughts overwhelmed and tormented her. In a nutshell, by offering to share her room with him, Selena had scared herself silly.

She was nervous. She couldn't sit still. Yet, on the other hand, she felt conspicuous when she got up to pace the small lounge area. Her palms were wet. Her throat was dry. Her heart beat like a kettledrum. And she felt light-headed.

Selena started every time the elevator doors swished open, and sighed with relief each time he failed to step out. She was telling herself that she really didn't have to follow through with her offer when the doors slid apart and Luke was suddenly there, beckoning her.

Upstairs, Luke had rapidly washed, shaved, brushed his teeth and hair, and changed his shirt. That was all, but it was way beyond enough. He gleamed with health—and the promise of an exciting evening ahead.

"Ready?" Selena put on a smile and briskly strode for the door. Her step faltered slightly when his murmured answer caught up to her.

"For anything."

To Selena, Luke's "anything" meant everything— everything she had avoided throughout her adult life. *Commitment of the flesh.*

The phrase crept into her mind as Luke stepped in front of her to open the door for her. The shiver feathering her bare shoulders and arms owed nothing to the light breeze scenting the mild evening.

Was she seriously contemplating sharing herself, her body, with this man? Selena asked herself, giving him an absent smile of thanks as she walked by him. When push came to shove, could she go through with it? Musing, she automatically followed the walkway through the hotel courtyard and onto the River Walk.

The answer came with a rush of recent memory. For an instant, Selena could feel the pressure of Luke's mouth against her own, could taste his unique flavor. Oh, yes, if push came to shove, she could go through with it. And, because of her precipitous offer, she was convinced that push would definitely come to shove before the night was over.

"Which way?"

Luke's question startled Selena out of her unsettling introspection. "Oh! Uh...this way!" She indicated the direction with a vague hand movement. "But since you're so hungry, I thought we could take a river taxi to save time."

Luke frowned. "A river taxi?"

"Yes." Selena glanced up, then down, the river. "There are boats, like barges, on the river. You can buy a ticket and...there's one now." She waved to indicate the craft negotiating the curve along the river. "I thought we could ride down to where the restaurants are, then walk back after dinner, if you like."

"I like." Luke smiled. "Where do we buy the tickets?"

Selena didn't answer—she couldn't answer, she was too busy fighting the melting effects of his warm smile. She flicked her hand to point out a landing located a short distance from the hotel.

"Then let's do it." Taking her hand, Luke struck out for the landing.

Let's do it. His innocuous remark set fire to Selena's imagination, causing a molten flow of sensation to every pulse point in her body. Doing *it* was all she could think about—and *it* had nothing to do with a boat ride or dinner. Her palm tingled in reaction to his skin against hers as she paced beside him, buffeted by conflicting winds of trepidation and anticipation.

The boat was full. The ride was short. Selena didn't notice. Every ounce of her attention was centered on the rough hand wrapped around hers and the man that hand belonged to. Luke asked questions. She answered them. She only hoped her replies made sense, because she didn't have a clue about what she was telling him.

"What about this place?"

Selena blinked and focused on the restaurant Luke was pointing at. Recognizing the establishment she nodded. "I've eaten in there," she said, successfully gathering what was left of her wits. "The food's good and the prices are fair."

"Steak?" Luke arched his eyebrows.

Selena laughed. "Yes."

"Well, then, let's get our feet on the ground."

Excellent advice, in more ways than one, Selena told herself.

The restaurant was doing a brisk business, but the hostess said they could be seated immediately if they had no objection to dining indoors. The patio overlooking the river seemed to be the preference of the majority of waiting patrons.

Selena left the decision to Luke, who shrugged. They were seated at once inside the dining room.

The menus were huge. Luke barely glanced at his, and Selena hid a smile behind hers. He ordered a steak, rare. She decided on blackened fish.

The restaurant had an old-world ambiance and an unhurried attitude. Dinner was to be savored and enjoyed, and the tension slowly eased from Selena's taut, expectant body.

"You're very quiet this evening," Luke observed, giving her a sober look over the soup appetizer.

"I'm tired," she explained, lowering her eyes to her steaming gumbo. "I didn't get much sleep last night."

She sipped the broth, then looked up in time to see him scowl.

"Why not?"

The underlying hardness in Luke's tone confused her. Watching him warily, Selena finished her soup before answering. "I drove most of the night."

Luke slid his soup plate aside, then broke a roll in a way that gave Selena the shivers. "Most of the night?" His tone was soft, silky with suspicion. "Why?"

Tension began uncurling inside her again. Impatient with him and with her own reactions, she forced herself to relax. "Why?" she repeated. "Because I didn't leave my house until after three-thirty this morning, that's why!"

"Three-thirty!" he exclaimed.

"Yes, three-thirty." His astonished expression threw Selena off balance. What difference could it possibly make to him what time she'd left? Frowning, she bit into the piece of butter-slathered roll he offered her. "Why?"

Luke hesitated, his frown mirroring hers, before a shadow of movement rippled his shoulders in a care-less-looking shrug. "Three-thirty just seems like an odd time to begin a journey."

Selena nibbled on the roll. "I really hadn't planned on taking a journey," she replied at length. "It was one of those spur-of-the moment decisions."

"I see," Luke muttered, sitting back as the waiter served their entrées. "Spur-of-the-moment, huh?"

Selena nodded. "Yes. Like yours."

His serrated knife sliced through the steak and made a grating noise against his plate. "What do you mean, like mine?"

"There's no reason to get testy! I thought you'd said that your decision to come to San Antonio had been spur-of-the-moment."

"Oh. Yeah." Luke stared at her for a second. Then he grinned. "I guess it was."

Thoroughly confused, Selena gave up the verbal battle. "Ah . . . how's your steak?"

"Great," Luke mumbled around the wedge he was chewing. "How's your fish?"

"Great," Selena echoed, positive it would have been if she were able to really taste it.

When her appetite was finally restored, she did enjoy the delicate flavor of the blackened fish and side dishes. The remainder of the meal was consumed in relative silence, giving proof of how very hungry they both were. Conversation resumed over after-dinner liqueurs and dark, rich coffee.

Then, appearing far too casual, Luke tossed his napkin aside and asked, "Are you too tired for a walk?"

"No." Selena heaved a sigh. "In fact, I believe a walk is required."

"Good." Standing, he held out his hand to her invitation. "You can introduce me to San Antonio."

Six

——

"This is the famous River Walk."

Luke gave Selena a dry look. They were standing outside the restaurant, staring at the river, which, as rivers go, wasn't exactly remarkable. "Cute." His tone reflected his expression. "This is my introduction to San Antonio?"

Selena offered him a bright, counterfeit smile. "It's a beginning."

"I've met this river," he reminded her. "I was on it less than two hours ago...remember?"

"But you haven't really seen it," Selena countered. "Have you?"

"Point taken." Luke glanced left, then right. "Pick a direction."

"This way." Selena turned right and began strolling along the crowded walkway.

Dodging the laughing, chattering pedestrian traffic, Luke strode to Selena's side. He shortened his step to align it with hers and clasped her hand. "I don't want to lose you," he said, curling his fingers around hers.

Selena felt the vibrations of his warm touch from her fingernails to her toenails. "Afraid you'll have to sleep on a bench somewhere if you do?" She tossed an arch look at him as she moved ahead to circle a group of dawdlers.

Luke's soft laughter tickled the back of her neck and her scalp and her ears. "No, I'm not afraid," he said, bringing her to his side with a light tug. "In case you haven't noticed, I've got you in tow." He lifted their clasped hands for her inspection.

Haven't noticed? She'd noticed little else since he'd wrapped his long hand around hers. She'd noticed the chills vying with the fire running rampant along her veins. She'd noticed the sudden constriction of her breath. She'd noticed the curling tendrils of fog clouding her mind. The only things she hadn't noticed were their surroundings and the people surging around them.

"I noticed," she confessed, willing a measure of carelessness into her tone. "Have you noticed any of the lure of the River Walk and the festive atmosphere?"

Luke's smile was conceived in erotic realms and born in his devilish eyes. His gaze fastened on her frowning face. "I noticed a definite lure," he said, lowering his eyes to her mouth. "But it has damn little to do with the river, the walk, the festive atmosphere or San Antonio.''

Selena's muscles contracted, and Luke's smile told her that he felt the clench. She cleared her throat and laughed. She had an overwhelming urge to leap into the river—if only to cool the sheen of heat shimmering over her body. She had to do something, and quickly. If not the river, then something less drastic. With the strains of music from several strolling players lending background, she drew a breath and launched into a rapid tour-guide monologue about the River Walk.

"As you can see—'' Selena motioned to a foot bridge arching over the water "—the *Paseo del Rio*, or River Walk, is located one level below the downtown streets.''

While at the moment, my mind is one level below normal function.

"The River Walk is considered by many to be San Antonio's major visitor attraction and experience.''

At this instant, however, it's second only to Luke Branson.

"The river meanders its way several miles through the center of town between banks abundant with giant cypress trees, palms, tropical foliage and flowering shrubs.''

Not to mention the deadwood referred to as a brain inside my head.

"If you'll note,'' she continued in a desperate tone, "much of the route is bordered by hotels, restaurants, cabarets, sidewalk cafés, boutiques, and art and gift shops.''

While my mental terrain consists only of sexy images of a handsome, dark-souled man.

"You've already experienced the river taxis, which offer half-hour scenic cruises, and—" She broke off as Luke held up his free hand in a sign of surrender.

"Okay, I give up." Though he made an anguished face at her, he was laughing. "I'll look. I'll observe. I'll absorb. Only, please—will you shut up?"

Feeling foolish, yet suddenly lighthearted, Selena laughed with him. "You weren't enthralled?"

"More like numbed." He gave her fingers a gentle squeeze of denial.

"More like bored," she corrected him.

"Never." Luke's response was immediate and thrilling. "You couldn't bore me if you worked at it."

"Not even by reading aloud from the phone book?" Not quite able to believe the sense of easy camaraderie she now felt with him, Selena slid a sparkling glance his way.

"Well..." Luke drawled the word, grinning. "You're beautiful, and the sound of your voice does do strange and wonderful things to my libido, but..." His voice faded and his grin remained.

"But...?" she prompted, inordinately flattered by his remark.

"I wouldn't go as far as the phone book." The grin still tugged at his chiseled lips—and her imagination.

Selena laughed. All at once, teasing him was easy and fun.

From their first meeting two weeks ago, Luke had struck her as aloof, withdrawn, cynical and a loner. Which wasn't surprising, since most of the people she had met since coming to West Texas were loners by choice. But this evening, whether by accident or design, he was revealing warmer, more approachable facets of his character. Maybe his soul wasn't quite as dark as she'd thought.

Luke's soft laughter merged with hers, instilling inside Selena a comforting sensation of ease. That in itself was unusual, since she was never truly at ease in the company of any other man. The feeling both fascinated and astonished her, and she was examining it when his low-pitched voice drew her from her reverie.

"Where have you gone, Selena?"

Blinking, she cast him a look of puzzlement. "Gone? I don't understand."

"You've gone off somewhere inside yourself. Where?" Before she could reply, his lips tightened and his voice grew an edge. "Who are you thinking about? Manuel?"

Selena came to an abrupt halt. "Manuel?" Genuine surprise colored her tone. "Why in the world would I be thinking about Manuel?"

Supremely unconcerned with the crowds jostling for space to move around them, Luke stood in the center of the walk and stared into her startled eyes. "Why not?" he retorted. "Didn't you drive here with him from the party last night?"

"What?" Sheer amazement raised her voice to a squeak. "What are you talking about?"

Luke didn't answer. "And didn't you spend the night with him in a motel in Alpine?" he went on in a relentless tone.

Because it was so sudden, so unexpected, his attack devastated Selena. A lethal mixture of emotions rocketed through her. She felt disappointment because his arrogant tone had wiped away her sense of ease and camaraderie. And she felt unutterably weary, because she had offered him something she had never before offered to a man—a glimpse of her true self— and he had thrown that offering in her face.

Selena's reaction would have been a subtle warning to anybody who knew her. Her small body grew rigid. Her delicate chin lifted and tilted. Her green eyes sparkled like emeralds reflecting a blazing noon sun. Her voice was as cold as the North Atlantic in January.

"I beg your pardon?"

Luke felt the chill to the depths of his overheated outrage. He had blundered badly, and he knew it. This cat-witch woman did not appreciate questions of a personal nature. She arched her back. She bristled. She unsheathed her claws. Luke was undone. She was so damned beautiful.

"Selena." His voice was low, calm, yet even he could hear the thread of a plea woven through the fabric of control.

"Answer me, damn you!"

Heads turned among the passersby, startled by her harsh note of command. Luke registered and ignored the curious glances sent their way. Denying an itch in his palm to stroke her, soothe her, he met her glaring green eyes with a dark, direct stare of his own and answered her with unadorned, unrepentant bluntness.

"I asked if you spent last night in bed with Manuel." Unaware of holding his breath, and fully expecting an explosion, Luke waited for her reaction. When it came, he was thrown completely off balance.

"That's what I thought you asked." The harshness had disappeared from Selena's voice, replaced by a remote, careless note. A small, weary smile curved her mouth. Jerking her hand free of his grasp, she turned and walked away from him. Her head was held high. Her back was straight. But he could see the betraying shake of her shoulders.

Cursing himself for shattering the harmonious accord they had been sharing, Luke strode after her. It was only when he reached out to clasp her arm that he realized her shoulders weren't shaking from unspent rage, but with uncontrollable inner amusement. She was silently laughing.

"Selena?" Luke peered at her, concerned. "Are you all right?"

"Manuel!" Selena exclaimed on a whoop. "That's really very funny!"

"It is?"

She brought her laughter under control with obvious effort. "Well, of course it is, you potato-head!"

Unappreciative of the unflattering name, Luke repeated, "Potato-head?"

Selena's bare shoulders quivered with laughter. "Only a potato-head would . . . Oh!" She gasped as a distracted tourist careened into her.

"Watch it, buddy!" Luke's voice cracked like a smartly uncoiled whip.

The startled man froze, then stammered an apology, inching along the walk to get away from the scowling Luke.

It was simply too much for Selena. Covering her laughing mouth with one hand, she grabbed Luke with the other. "We're blocking traffic." She began to walk, only to be brought up short by an immovable object . . . one Luke Branson.

His features set into hard lines of determination, his booted feet planted on the walk, Luke stood like a statue and looked every bit as solid and unyielding. "I'm not going anywhere until you explain why only a potato-head would—" He broke off to give her an implacable stare.

"Oh, for heaven's sake, Luke! Lighten up!" Selena laughed. "It was only an expression."

"I'm glad you're amused." His steely tone told her that glad was the last thing he was feeling.

Heaving a tired, telling sigh, Selena just looked at him and shook her head. "What a grouch," she muttered, glancing around the area. "Look—" she indicated a nearby sidewalk cabaret with a flick of her hand "—I'm tired and I'm thirsty. Let's get out of the way here. I promise I'll explain myself over a drink. Okay?" She gave him a coaxing smile, along with a gentle tug on his hand.

"Okay." Luke allowed her to draw him along the walkway and up the steps to the large porch of the cabaret. "But this had better be good."

The place was jammed, inside and out, with people ranging in age from late teens to senior citizens, all of whom appeared to be hell-bent on having a good time.

There was one empty table, a tiny one, against the slatted railing in the curve of the porch. Another young couple was heading for the table from inside the building. Moving like quicksilver, Luke snaked through the crowd, beating the other couple to the table by a hair.

The other man glared at Luke.

Drawing himself up to his full height, Luke turned on the ice and glared back.

The man retreated.

Selena was forced to turn away to hide her once-again uncontrollable laughter. Her entire body shook with it. She could barely choke out her preference for white wine to the waitress who approached the table.

"Are you having fun?" Luke asked in a muttered growl when the waitress departed.

Swinging around, Selena laughed in his face. "As a matter of fact, I am." She held her breath, waiting for his reaction, wondering if he'd see the humor in the situation.

For a long, disappointing moment, Luke stared at her. Then, to her utter relief, he exhaled a deep breath and grinned at her.

It was amazing. One grin from him and the tension was gone, the camaraderie restored. Selena moved automatically when he pulled out a chair and motioned for her to sit down. She watched as he settled his length on the chair opposite her, and she felt a pang in her heart when his grin slipped into a self-derisive smile.

"Okay, I'm behaving like a jerk." His shoulders rippled in a shrug, drawing her fascinated gaze to the muscles flexing beneath the smooth cotton of his shirt. "I'm sorry." His chiseled mouth twisted into a grimace. "I was out of line," he admitted. "You had every right to call me a potato-head because I had no right at all questioning your actions." His voice went low, weighted by acceptance. "And I'll understand if you tell me to take a hike and find my own room for the night."

Selena was tempted, not because she was afraid of him, but because she was afraid of the liquefying effect he was having on her. She drew a breath, smiled and drew another before she found her voice and the words to respond to him.

"I'm not going to tell you to take a hike, Luke."

His relief was visible and flattering. But a tiny frown line still marred his brow. "Thank you, but maybe you've spoken too soon." He glanced up, murmuring thanks as the waitress set their drinks on the table.

"What do you mean?" She sipped her wine.

"I must ask one more question."

Her eyebrows arched. "And that is?"

He hesitated, then plunged. "I could understand your anger," he said. "But why were you laughing?"

"Because I met Manny this afternoon when I arrived at the hotel," Selena explained with a laugh. "He works there." She took another, larger sip from her glass.

Luke's expression went blank. "Works there?"

"Yes," she said. "He's one of the desk clerks. He was on duty when I arrived. I had come down from my room tonight a moment before you strolled into the lobby. Manny was just going off duty and stopped to chat for a few seconds."

The look that transformed Luke's features was both sheepish and shrewd. Studying her, he took a deep swallow of the beer he'd ordered. "You're right, I acted like a potato-head," he conceded. "But you were also wrong."

"In what way?" Selena demanded.

"I saw the look in Manny's eyes," Luke said dryly. "He was devouring you. Believe me, a casual chat with you was the last thing on his mind."

Since Selena had reached the exact same conclusion at the time, she could hardly argue the point. She had known what was wriggling around inside Manny's mind as well as she knew what was fermenting inside Luke's gray matter. A teasing, knowing light sparked a fire in her green eyes.

"Are you accusing Manny of having the same kind of designs on my person that you have yourself?" she asked in a sweetly barbed tone.

"Yes, damn him!" Luke retorted with blunt honesty. His dark eyes pierced hers. "You may as well know that I intend to have you, to make you mine."

A thrill slid down the length of Selena's spine, then shot back to her neck like a bolt of heat lightning. Luke wasn't pulling his punches, and she determined that she wouldn't fudge, either. "I know," she said, meeting his drilling stare over the rim of her glass. Feeling a sudden need for fortification, she drained the wine before continuing, "And you may as well know that, before leaving Alpine this morning, I decided to take you for my first lover."

* * *

Her bald statement stopped Luke's mental train in its tracks. His thoughts fractured, shooting out in several directions at once.

First lover?

The phrase revolved inside his rattled mind. What did she mean by "first lover"? Surely she wasn't a...? Nah, he thought, dismissing the idea. If he was any judge at all, Selena had to be pushing thirty. Beyond her age and by her own admission, Selena had been working on one or another river for some years, thrown into the company of a variety of different men. The situation didn't lend itself to celibacy.

So, scratch the *first* business.

But—lover?

A delicious tingle danced on the surface of Luke's body, while a near-painful tightness invaded his insides. Selena had said that she had decided to take him for her lover. His thoughts condensed into one overriding question.

When?

It required every ounce of control Luke possessed to keep himself from leaping up, grabbing her by the hand and sprinting back to the hotel. Instead, suddenly drier than the Texas desert, he chugged his beer and motioned to the waitress for refills.

What was he thinking?

Wishing for another drink to ease the sudden parched feeling in her throat, Selena watched the man seated opposite her, searching his expressionless face.

Luke didn't reveal a hint of what he was thinking or feeling.

The noise level around them was intense. Laughter, animated conversation and merriment abounded. Music blared from inside as well as outside the establishment. Selena didn't hear any of it. All her concentration was centered on the silent man she had just invited to be her lover.

Lover.

Selena shivered. Was she crazy or what? He probably thought she was at best, forward, and at worst, easy.

The waitress delivered fresh drinks. Selena pounced on hers like her very life depended upon the chilled wine. Without the liberating spirit, she wasn't certain that she'd have the nerve to go through with her invitation.

The silence lengthened between them, stretching Selena's nerves to the twitching stage. Her glass was empty, her mind was empty, her body was a mass of quivering sensations.

Disjointed thoughts ricocheted through her head, making her even more uneasy.

Why didn't Luke say something—anything?

Why had she started this?

Why didn't she take to the hills?

"Why are you so uptight?"

Selena's body jerked at the low sound of Luke's voice. She blinked, swallowed, then blinked again. After waiting forever for him to comment, she didn't know how to respond now that he had. "Ah..." She cleared her throat and raked her mind for a coherent reply. Her mind was dry—and so was her throat. "I . . . er, I'd like another drink, please."

His smile should have been registered with the authorities as a lethal weapon, and his dark eyes sent messages that would have been banned in Boston. Luke raised his hand to catch their waitress's attention. "Relax, Selena," he murmured in a sexy drawl. "There's no reason for you to be anxious. We're going to be very good together."

"Or very bad." Clapping a hand over her mouth, Selena stared at him in wide-eyed disbelief. Had she actually blurted her thought aloud? The sudden flare of desire leaping in his eyes, his burst of soft laughter, gave her the discouraging proof that she had.

"I think I like your assessment better." He raised his beer can in a silent salute, then tossed back the remaining contents. And not a moment too soon, as the waitress arrived at the table to deposit fresh drinks.

Concentrating on appearing casual, Selena picked up her glass and brought it to her lips. The cool wine trickled down her throat, then went straight to her head. A rosy glow enveloped her. Her eyelids grew heavy. Observing Luke through mellowed vision, she felt a curl of excitement deep inside at the movement of his mouth as he talked to the waitress. His mouth was so alluring in its unrelenting, clean, masculine line. But then, she mused fuzzily, everything about the entire six feet odd inches of him was appealing. And not only to her, apparently.

Narrowing her eyes, Selena shifted her attention to the smiling, flustered waitress. What had Luke said to make the woman preen like a peacock? She gathered her wits to focus on their exchange.

What Selena heard sent a tremor down her spine. Luke had asked for the check—which meant he wouldn't be ordering any more drinks—which meant they would be leaving the cabaret when their drinks were finished—which meant they would be going back to the hotel—which meant...

Selena took a deep swallow from her glass.

"Hey, Green Eyes, take it easy." Luke's tone was teasing. "You don't want to risk drowning the inner fire—do you?"

Staring into the blazing depths of his eyes, Selena slowly shook her head. "No." With the murmured admission came the realization that it was true. She didn't want to drown the inner fire. The wine had performed its duty. With each successive sip, she had felt her inhibitions fall away, exposing the essence of her womanhood, revealing every deeply buried desire. And she desired Luke with every fiber of her being. Defenseless against her sudden need of him, she was beyond concealing it from him. "No," she repeated in a voice made husky by passion. "I don't want to drown the fire."

A hissing sound accompanied Luke's indrawn breath. He went still, staring at her, her eyes, her mouth, her flushed soft skin. Then he moved. Scraping back his chair, he surged to his feet and held out his hand to her. He didn't say a word—words were unnecessary.

Selena carefully set her glass on the table before sliding her palm over his. The touch was light, the friction electrifying. Willing to follow wherever he might lead, she went to his side.

As they stepped off the porch and onto the River Walk, Luke curled his arm around her waist. Without hesitation, she reciprocated. In silent accord, they strolled arm in arm to the hotel.

The combined effects of too little rest and too much wine caught up to Selena in the hotel elevator. She blinked and stifled a yawn. Her eyelids began to droop as she paced beside Luke along the corridor to her room. She tightened her grip around his waist. Her eyes drifted shut as he inserted the key in the lock. Surrendering, she sighed and snuggled into the curve of his neck.

"Are you all right?" Luke's warm breath caressed her cheek—and her sensibilities.

"Yes," she whispered, then moaned "No."

His arm tightened. The door swung open. His voice held comforting concern. "What's wrong?"

Selena roused herself enough to turn her pouting mouth up to him. "I need a kiss."

He met her demand with immediate action. Drawing her into the room, Luke slammed the door and swept her around into his arms. His mouth captured her parted lips, while his hands molded her soft curves to his own hard angles. With gentle manipulation, he pried her lips farther apart with his. His tongue speared into her mouth. She felt the piercing sweetness in the core of her femininity.

A confusing mixture of weakness and strength shimmered through Selena. Raising her arms, she encircled his taut neck, then clung to him to keep from folding like a fan and collapsing onto the floor.

"Selena."

He groaned her name into her mouth. She heard it with inflamed senses, and responding to the unspoken plea, she tentatively stroked his tongue with the tip of her own. The touch affected Luke like a blast from a torch. The muscles in his arms flexed convulsively, crushing her against him. His mouth plundered hers. He began to move, slowly, inexorably, toward the bed.

Although her legs moved in step with him, Selena didn't feel the floor beneath her feet. She was floating. The sensation was heady, exciting. A light jolt brought her down to earth when the back of her legs made contact with the foot of the bed. He lifted his mouth from hers. She murmured a throaty protest and opened her eyes.

"I'm sleepy."

"No, you're not." Luke's lowered voice was a feral growl. His hands tugged the blouse from the waistband of her skirt. An instant later, the garment skimmed over her head and into the air, forgotten before it landed in the corner. The cool air bathed her flushed torso.

"I'm not?" She shivered, not from the air conditioning, but in response to his palms stroking her bare skin. Following an impish urge, she outlined his mouth with the moist tip of her tongue. "What am I then?"

Luke's breath came in harsh, uneven gasps. "You're beautiful, playful and sexy as hell." His fingers found the front clasp of her strapless bra and released it with one expert movement. The fabric fell away and he filled his hands with her warm, vibrant flesh. "And you're driving me crazy."

Sexy as hell? Her? Selena was enchanted with the idea. Her unpleasant experiences with men had led her to believe that all her natural sensuality had been extinguished. Had she been wrong? Testing, she set her fingers to work on the buttons of his shirt. Luke assisted her, shrugging it from his shoulders when the last of the buttons were free. She touched him. His skin was warm, surprisingly smooth, and she felt the reflexive tremor that rippled through his body.

"God, Selena, I want you!" His fingers released the button at the waist of her skirt. It slid unnoticed to the carpet. "I can taste the wanting."

Encouraged by his confession, she lowered her head to his chest, and his wiry hair there tickled her nose. She inhaled. His special scent clouded her mind. "I'd rather you tasted me," she admitted, pressing her lips to his salty-flavored skin. "You taste..."

"Good?" he asked when she hesitated.

"Erotic," she whispered, closing her lips around one flat male nipple.

Luke groaned.

Selena laughed.

"Selena." Grasping her around the waist, Luke pressed her down until she was seated on the very edge of the bed. Then, to her amazement, he dropped to the floor in front of her. Kneeling between her parted thighs, he cupped her aching breasts and lowered his head to bury his face in the perfume-scented valley.

Pressing against her, he took her back and down to the mattress.

"Luke." Selena was on fire, burning with a desire she understood on an intellectual level, but had never before experienced in a physical sense. Obeying ancient dictates, she reached for the clasp on his jeans. The zipper made a jagged, whirring noise in the quiet room. "I want . . ."

"I know." Leaning back, away from her, he helped her yank the pants and underbriefs over his clenched buttocks and down his passion-hardened flanks. "I want, too." Surging forward, he arched his body into hers.

Selena welcomed his advance with enfolding, silken thighs. But a tiny triangle of satin held firm against his invasion. Through her panties, she could feel the power of him. The sensation drove her wild. She reached for the lace-covered elastic connecting the swatches of cloth, but Luke was faster, surer. The elastic snapped. The triangle fell to the bed.

"Now." His voice was hoarse.

"Yes." Her voice was nearly nonexistent.

Drawing a breath, Luke clasped her hips, raised her from the mattress and thrust forward—into virgin territory.

The pain was not unexpected, but shocking nonetheless. Selena was unable to smother an involuntary outcry or control the stiffening of her body.

"Selena?" Fused and frozen within her, Luke stared down at her in astonished disbelief.

Her eyes were closed and she didn't answer. She was too busy concentrating on taking slow, regular breaths.

"Selena!" Impatience tinged his concerned tone.

She drew a final long, deep breath. The pain was gone. The tension eased from her body. But the heat remained. "Yes?" She opened her eyes and smiled at him.

"You're a virgin!"

Her smile curved into an enticing line. A gleam lit her eyes. "Not anymore."

"But—" he began.

Selena silenced him by lifting her hands to clasp his face. Wantonly, she drew his mouth to hers. "No buts," she whispered against his lips. "It's time for us to be very good and very bad . . . together."

Seven

"**B**elieve it or don't!"

Selena tossed a wry look at her companion. "Believe it or don't?" she repeated in a matching wry tone.

The teasing smile curving Luke's mouth and gleaming in his eyes shot straight to her senses. Luke's mouth. Hunger caused a hollow feeling inside her, a clawing emptiness unrelated to food. Positive her craving was blatantly evident to him, she returned her gaze to the building bearing the large sign he had jokingly misquoted. The sign read: Plaza Theater of Wax and Ripley's Believe It Or Not.

They were standing on the sidewalk near the attraction located directly across the wide boulevard from the Alamo. It was still early and the famous shrine was not yet open to the public. But the tourist attraction, billed as the Ultimate Adventure, had just opened for business.

"Have you been in to see it?" Luke spoke close to her ear, sending a warm wave of awareness crashing through her.

"No." Her braid swung back and forth as she shook her head, reminding her of the dexterous motion of Luke's fingers as he'd plaited her hair earlier that morning. Even now, over three hours later, the memory retained the power to set her senses leaping in anticipation.

"Well," he said when it became obvious that she wasn't going to elaborate. "Would you like to see it?"

Reacting to the effervescent feeling flowing through her, Selena slanted a grin at him. "Believe it or not...I would. Would you?"

Luke volleyed the grin back to her. "It's here. I'm here. Why not?" Stepping forward, he pulled the door open and with an exaggerated sweep of his arm, ushered her inside.

They decided to do the wax museum first. It was divided into three sections, consisting of a Hollywood section, a horror section and a history section.

Hands clasped, they ambled through the exhibition, exchanging impressions of the wax scenes with the ease of old friends and confidants.

"I saw that silent movie on TV!" Selena exclaimed, staring in delight at a scene from *The Phantom of the Opera*. "That wax figure is incredible. It looks exactly like Lon Chaney did in the film."

"It does, at that," Luke agreed, tugging on her hand to keep her moving. "There's Duke," he said a moment later, tilting his head to study the scene depicting John Wayne as he had appeared in the role of Hondo. "I had a severe case of hero worship for Wayne when I was a kid."

"Didn't everyone?" Selena asked. She was somehow positive that the tough, individualistic characters John Wayne portrayed had appealed to the strength of Luke's own budding personality.

He smiled at her. "You liked him too, huh?"

"Sure," she admitted. "Wayne and Gary Cooper and Gregory Peck and him." She inclined her head to indicate the imposing wax figure of Charlton Heston attired in the garb of a Roman, standing tall and victorious in a chariot. "More recently," she went on as they moved along, "Clint Eastwood has entered the fold." She gave Luke a sparkling, revealing glance. "I always was a pushover for the strong, silent type."

"You!" he exclaimed, laughing. "Selena, you are the last woman I'd describe as being a pushover."

"It's true, though, in a way," she insisted, continuing on to the next display.

She had been a virgin, which proved Luke's point. On the other hand, Selena suddenly understood why she had felt such an immediate strong attraction to him. From the moment she had walked into the tour office to find him propped against the counter, Luke had appeared to be the living representation of her childhood heroes. And it hadn't been the actors she admired as much as the personality traits of the characters they portrayed.

With startling clarity, Selena realized that she was still a pushover for the strong, silent type—the rare breed that was quiet but self-reliant, confident, competent, dependable, larger than life. And, until Luke appeared on the scene, her virginity and emotions had been safe because she had believed her secret concept of the ideal man was merely the stuff of dreams and fantasies.

"You seem to personify every quality I have ever admired in the characters these actors played on the screen," she told Luke.

He reacted to her remark without a hint of warning or sound. Releasing her hand, he slid one arm around her waist and drew her into the shadowed corner of a display, out of sight of the people trailing several yards behind them. Before Selena could even gasp in surprise, he pulled her into his arms and crushed her mouth with his.

The world tilted, her mind spun off into space and Selena was immediately flung back in time, to the darkness of the night and the hours of their wild, sweet loving.

"It's time for us to be very good and very bad... together."

The results of Selena's enticing invitation had been breathtaking, shattering in intensity.

Luke literally sprang to life. Selena felt the power of him leap deep within her body. Excitement shimmered through her as, emitting a low, hungry growl, he claimed her mouth and her body, with his. His plundering tongue reflected the motion of his more complete possession of her.

His hands were everywhere, seemingly at once—in her hair, on her face, encircling her throat, cupping her breasts, stroking her thighs, cradling her hips.

Sensation topping sensation, freeing her mind, releasing inhibitions, Selena clung to him, arched for him, moved with him as, driving, driving, Luke propelled his magnificent body deeper, ever deeper, straining in an agony of pleasure toward the ultimate sensual experience.

His breathing harsh, his voice even harsher, Luke murmured words of encouragement. "Yes, yes, Green Eyes, let yourself go, give in to your desires."

Her voice little more than a gasping whisper, Selena responded in kind. "I want to... I have to! Help me, tell me, show me, kiss me... hard!"

He took her mouth with savage sweetness, drinking from her while quenching her own raging thirst. Their tongues twined, stroked, then twined again, sharpening their pleasure to an almost painful degree.

"You're beautiful." His fingers traced her facial features. "Here." He filled his hands with her quivering breasts. "And here." His palms glided over her flat belly. "And here." His fingers tangled in the tight cluster of black curls at the apex of her thighs. "And here."

"And you're wonderful!" Selena exclaimed on a strangled gasp. "But you're driving me mad!"

Luke's laughter rumbled, deep inside his heaving chest. "I sincerely hope so." The tip of his tongue meandered down her arched throat. "I'm working at it."

"Luke, please..." Her voice fading to a moan, Selena clutched at his taut flanks, seeking an anchor to keep her from soaring away from him.

"What?" Maintaining the rapid rhythm of his body, Luke lowered his head to suckle at her breast. "What do you want that I'm not giving to you?"

Barely aware of what she was saying, Selena moved her head in denial. "Nothing...I mean...I can't bear it. The tension...it's too much. I can't... Oh!" she cried out as he increased the rocking tempo.

"You can. You will." Arching over her like a pillar of flame, Luke stared into her face, feeding his own passion by looking at hers. "You're so soft, so silky." His hands skimmed over her body from her shoulders to her ankles to the satin smoothness of her inner thighs. "Outside." Drawing a ragged breath, he thrust deeper within her. "And inside."

Breath suspended, exhilaration warring with exhaustion inside her, Selena sank her nails into his flesh and arched into his plunging body.

In the throes of acute arousal, Luke's face was drawn, a study in intense passion and iron control. Feeling a sense of elation and power, Selena realized she was the instrument of his obvious pleasure. In her euphoric sensuously saturated opinion, he had never looked more handsome, or more devilish.

"Luke...Luke!" The cry was wrenched from Selena's throat as her inner tension reached fever pitch.

"Hang on!" he gasped. "One...more...moment!" His fingers bit into her hips as he surged forward. "Now!"

The invisible cord snapped, flinging Selena into a cascading maelstrom of pulsating sensation. She heard her own cry of exaltation echoed by Luke's triumphant shout.

Conquered yet victorious and thoroughly spent, Selena lay curled within the haven of Luke's embrace, positive the ecstatic experience would be impossible to duplicate.

But it was happening again. She was on fire for him, burning for him. Forgetting where they were, Selena raked her fingers through Luke's hair and returned his kiss with voracious fervor.

Obviously aroused by her touch, Luke inserted his leg between her thighs. The rough material of his jeans abraded the skin exposed below the hem of her shorts. The feeling was delicious, sending shards of excitement streaking to the recently awakened and sensitized core of her being. Without thought, caution or consideration, Selena parted her legs in a silent invitation to him to step inside.

Deepening the kiss, Luke brought his hard body into contact with hers. Bubbles of sensation exploded inside her and Selena moaned a protest against their confining clothing, arching with a convulsive need of more of him.

"Oh, my goodness!" The surprised-sounding female voice pierced the haze clouding Selena's mind. "Ladies, I think we must visit the rest room."

Luke was shaking with laughter when he released her mouth and set her from him. "Very accommodating of them." He jerked his head to indicate the hasty retreat of the three matrons who had been trailing them through the museum.

"And very indiscreet of us," Selena muttered. Appalled and embarrassed by her behavior, she averted her face and spun away from him.

"Selena, wait." Snagging her wrist with his long fingers, Luke brought her up short. "Why are you so rattled?" Though his expression was bland, his eyes fairly danced with inner amusement. "It was only a kiss."

"No," she said in sharp denial. "It was not only a kiss. It was a display more blatant and vivid than any of these, here in the museum." A flick of her hand indicated her assertion. "It was also juvenile," she continued, stalking blindly along the section devoted to historical scenes. "The kind of exhibition put on by teenagers who want to be noticed."

"All that?" Luke asked. "And here I was, thinking it was nothing more than a friendly kiss."

He was deliberately taunting her, trying to tease her out of her disconcerted mood. Selena knew it, and yet she couldn't control her emotional response. "Nothing more than a friendly kiss, my foot!" she exclaimed, coming to a dead stop and staring at him in astonishment. "Luke Branson! We were all over each other! Why, if it hadn't been for those women, in another moment we'd have been tearing our clothes off and—" She broke off, her face flaming in response to the explicitly erotic images flashing into her mind.

"And . . . what?" he asked in a silky drawl.

"You know damned well what," Selena retorted, turning away from his knowing eyes. Agitated and abashed beyond endurance, she strode from the historical section and down the stairway leading to the horror section.

"I wouldn't have let it go that far," Luke called after her in a tone of reassuring conviction.

I would have.

Keeping the revealing acknowledgment to herself, Selena pushed through the doors into the horror section of the museum. Luke caught up to her before the doors squeaked shut behind her.

"Look, Green Eyes, nothing happened," he said in a soothing tone. "So we had a hot kiss and an audience." He captured her hand and laced his fingers through hers. "So what? It probably made their week."

Tugging futilely against his grip, Selena shot a fuming look at him. "You really think this is all very amusing . . . that *I'm* very amusing, don't you?" she demanded. She was so upset by her own emotional conflict that she hardly noticed the shrieks, rattles and bangs that were the sound effects of the section.

"I think you're making too much of it," Luke replied, glancing with disinterest at a rather gory display. "We just happen to have discovered that we turn each other on something fierce." He shrugged. "It's as simple as that."

Unable to refute the first part of his assertion with any degree of honesty, Selena pounced on the second part. "The only simple thing about it is that it was simpleminded," she snapped, pushing through the doors leading out of the section. "We are supposedly two mature, intelligent adults," she went on, mounting the broad stairs that led to street level.

"And mature, intelligent adults never get the hots?" Luke asked with amazement.

In the spacious lobby at the top of the stairs, Selena turned on him, hands on her hips, her green eyes flashing fire. "How should I know? I've never..." Her voice deserted her at the sight of his complacent expression.

"I know you've never," he murmured in the same silky tone he'd used before. "I've been in a position to know." His smile was suggestive. "If you'll recall?"

If she'd recall? She hadn't been able to do anything all morning *but* recall the position he had been in, not once, but twice since they'd returned to the hotel last night. And the recollection was not only wreaking havoc on her senses and turning her into a veritable basket case—it was undermining and eroding her self-image. Having taken great pride in believing that she was above the sexuality that directed the actions of others around her, Selena was having a difficult time accepting her surrender to him—and to the clamoring dictates of her own newly-discovered sensuality.

"Se—lee—na." Luke's soft call and the gentle yank he gave her braid scattered her reverie.

She had been quiet too long. He was waiting for a response to his question, waiting for her to admit to her own susceptibility. The devil. How could she answer? What could she say... other than the obvious? He had her cornered and she knew it. What was worse—he knew it. The unvarnished truth was tainted by the taste of humble pie.

"Yes," she muttered, lowering her eyes to the brightly patterned lobby carpet. "I recall."

"Believe It or Not."

His drawled remark brought her head up with a snap. "What did you say?"

"The exhibition." Luke flicked his hand to indicate the banner above the entrance. "Since I've paid the admission price, don't you think we may as well go in?"

"Oh!" Selena glanced from him to the banner, then back to him. With sudden insight, she realized that by changing the subject, Luke was offering her a reprieve, time to collect herself. "Oh…yes! Of course." In return, she offered him a faint, whimsical smile. "But, Luke, please—no more dark corners or hot kisses in public."

Luke was fighting a laugh—but he was losing the battle. His lips twitched, then parted. It was no use, try as he would, he couldn't repress the sense of good spirits that had been with him all morning. His soft laughter erupted as he held out his hand to her. "Then let's go."

At any other time, Luke knew, he would have been fascinated by the assortment of odd and interesting articles and facts. But on this particular morning, his concentration was limited, focused entirely on Selena and the events that had occurred since he'd arrived in San Antonio.

Had he thought she was beautiful? Luke mused, compulsively stroking the pad of his thumb over the warm skin on the back of her hand. He had been wrong. Beautiful wasn't nearly comprehensive enough. Of course, in face and form, Selena was beautiful, but she was also so much more than merely that. Selena was ... was ...

His thumb stroking, stroking, Luke glanced at her, then around at the displays, while inwardly searching for a word or words to describe her. A smile curved his lips when he glanced absently at a sign and saw the perfect word, right there in bold-face letters.

Unbelievable.

Yes, Luke decided. In regard to Selena, *unbelievable* said it all.

She was unbelievably beautiful.

She was unbelievably her own person.

She was unbelievably exciting.

She was unbelievably sexy.

And he had never before felt so unbelievably satisfied—yet still hungry for the taste of her, the feel of her, the sheer joy of being one with her.

A tremor of arousal quaked through Luke's body, waking the sleeping tiger of need. He wanted to look at Selena. No, he wanted to kiss her. Hell, he wanted to be inside her, part of her, experiencing again the silky heat of her.

Moisture slicked Luke's brow and the nape of his neck. He was on fire. It was hellish. It was heavenly. It was confusing as the very devil.

What had—was—happening to him? Luke asked himself, applying considerable willpower to control the immediate response of his body. He had wanted other women, before and since he had been married. But never had he desired any woman as much as he desired Selena—including his former wife. What was it about this cat-witch woman, what was her appeal, what was the allure she possessed that turned him on so fiercely?

Though it was true that before last night he had been celibate for some months, Luke acknowledged without conceit that his celibacy had been self-imposed. His empty bed had not been due to disinterest on the part of the female sex, both since his relocation to West Texas six months ago and before leaving his home state of Pennsylvania.

If there was one thing Luke couldn't tolerate, it was an enigma. And for him, Selena McInnes was an enigma, a puzzle to be solved. Besides her obvious attributes—her beauty, her competence, her personality—she had been a virgin, for God's sake! Not even to himself could Luke deny the thrill that had streaked through him at his moment of discovery. There had been an instant of surprised shock, and then a wave of pure masculine satisfaction.

He was the first! Selena had been a virgin. But what a magnificent, wanton virgin. And she had admitted to choosing him because he possessed the qualities and characteristics she admired in a man! His muscles clenched in remembrance, forcing him to repeat the cool-mind-over-sensuous-performance.

And yet, supremely confident that once he had solved the mystery of her, his fascination would wane, Luke relished the challenge she presented.

He would have her, take everything she offered, as often and for as long as it took for him to decipher his attraction to her. And then he would walk away from the encounter, unscathed and untouched in any personal way, exactly as he had walked away from every woman since the bitter awakening of his divorce.

Eyes narrowed to conceal his thoughts and the raw desire smoldering in their depths, Luke sliced a glittering look at Selena. She was studying a wall decoration constructed entirely from chewing-gum wrappers. He was beginning to suspect the intensity of her stare when, as if she felt the heat and intent of his gaze, she raised her eyes to his.

"Hi."

Luke bit back a groan. One soft, tiny word and he could feel his cold, calculating theory sinking into the tide of emotions pooling in his throat.

Maybe, just maybe, walking away from Selena wouldn't be quite as easy as he'd believed it would be. Yet, either way, in that instant, Luke was determined to enjoy every moment, every nuance of their time together.

"Hi."

Luke's low, sexy-sounding response activated the liquefying mechanism inside Selena. Squashing an impulse to melt into his arms, she drew a deep breath and worked up a bright smile. "Seen enough?" she asked in a surprisingly normal tone, considering she felt decidedly abnormal. "The Alamo opened about fifteen minutes ago," she went on, heading for the exit. "Besides, I'm getting hungry."

Luke laughed, but allowed her to lead him out of the building. "How can you be hungry after the breakfast you demolished this morning?" he inquired in a teasing tone, falling into step beside her.

Selena gave him a look. "I can be hungry because of what occurred *after* breakfast this morning...if you'll recall?"

"Yeah," he drawled, grinning at her. "I recall giving you quite a workout."

Heat unrelated to the brazen Texas sun spread over Selena's cheeks and dried her throat. In an eternity of an instant, she relived their morning romp. She could taste the combined flavors of coffee and grape jam on his greedy mouth, could feel the imprint of his hard body crushing her softness into the mattress, experienced again the thrill of being joined with him in an ageless ritual.

Selena made a strangled sound deep in her throat. Luke's bark of laughter sent heat streaking to more southerly, sensitive regions of her body, reigniting fires of excitement and arousal.

This was getting ridiculous! Selena chastised herself, increasing her pace. Never in her life would she have believed it possible to feel such an intensity of physical and emotional awareness of any man. But with Luke, Selena had the uncanny sensation that she could actually feel the sting from the electrical charge sparking between them.

"Care to tell me where we're heading?"

"The Menger Hotel," Selena replied without faltering or breaking stride. She didn't need to see his head swivel around to know he was looking at her with eager anticipation.

"We're going to take a room?"

"We're going to have lunch," she retorted.

"In a room?" he persisted—pushing his luck.

"In the restaurant!" Selena exclaimed, at her wits' end as to how to cope with his amorous teasing. "They prepare a cheese soup there that's to die for."

"I'll be the judge of that."

Allowing a superior expression to speak for her, Selena didn't reply as she swept into the restaurant located in one corner of the old, elegant hotel.

But there was no escaping the tormenting gleam in Luke's eyes. He was having the time of his life teasing her, and his intention to continue in the same vein was apparent. Desperate to steer clear of the topic, Selena went into her tour-guide routine the moment their lunch order was taken by the pleasant Mexican-American waitress.

"A German brewer named W. A. Menger began building this hotel in 1858, just twenty-two years after the fall of the Alamo," she said in a blurted rush.

"Indeed?" Luke arched his eyebrows satanically and grinned at her knowingly.

"Yes, indeed." Selena gulped for breath, then hurried on. "This was the finest hotel on the frontier and has housed some famous historical people."

Luke sipped the steaming coffee the waitress had served while Selena was speaking and stared at her over the rim of his cup. "And you're going to tell me the names of every one of them, right?"

"Yes." Selena's smile was pure confection. "Or at least everyone that I can remember."

"I had a sneaky hunch you would."

"Chalk one up to your sneaky hunch."

Laughing, Luke set his cup on the table and settled back in his chair. "Okay, lay the history lesson on me."

Deciding he could be as devastating out of bed as he was in it, Selena laughed with him. "You promise you won't be bored?"

"Selena, I think I've already told you that you couldn't bore me if you worked at it," he said. "And you are working at it, aren't you?"

"It shows?" She fluttered her eyelashes.

Her display of exaggerated innocence broke him up. His roar of laughter drew smiles from nearby patrons. After he regained control, he stared at her in consternation and wonder. "You know, I just realized something," he said, frowning.

"And what's that?" Selena asked.

"I haven't laughed this much or enjoyed myself as much in years. You're fun to be with."

"Really?" She was melting again, but she didn't care. Pleased and flattered by his compliment, she lowered her eyes and murmured, "Thank you."

His eyes grew bright with the now-familiar devilish sheen. "In more ways than one."

Her eyes narrowed. The beast. He was doing it again, teasing her, tormenting her, making her aware of him, making her want him. Selena didn't know whether to laugh or throw her coffee cup at him. She did neither. Instead, she punished him with a historical recitation.

"Robert E. Lee was staying here when he was called back to Washington because tensions were heating up between the North and the South."

"You mean like things are heating up right now between you and me?"

"Luke!" Selena moaned, but plowed ahead. "Ulysses S. Grant also stayed at the Menger when he was in San Antonio, but he was not the only president to stay here. Taft, McKinley, Eisenhower and Nixon were guests here. The poet Sidney Lanier lived here for many years. You can book a room and request sleeping in a bed used by Oscar Wilde, Sarah Bernhardt, O. Henry, Lily Langtry, and many more."

"I'll take your word for it."

"Bored?"

"Never."

Leaning across the table, closer to him, Selena whispered, "Did you know the place is haunted?"

"No, I didn't know," Luke admitted, smiling at the waitress, who made no pretense of not listening as she served their food. "But I have a feeling I will before lunch is finished."

"A chambermaid by name of Sallie White was murdered here," Selena confided softly. "The murderer's identity remains unknown." She glanced to the left, then to the right and lowered her voice to a dramatic murmur. "They say that people with psychic powers have seen and heard poor Sallie walking the upper hallways."

"They?" Luke looked amused, and skeptical.

"It's true, *señor*," the waitress assured him, crossing herself. "I never go up there."

Calmly spooning soup into his mouth, Luke managed to contain himself until the waitress disappeared into the kitchen, then he fell apart. "Selena, you're priceless," he said between gasps for breath. "And you were also correct."

"Oh, how so?"

"I would have to agree that this cheese soup might be worth dying for," he said. "But I want to live to savor more satisfying lively moments with you."

Eight

"Jameson organized a nice piece of work on these fortifications," Luke said. His intent gaze studied the comprehensive model of the Alamo as it had appeared before the famous battle, displayed inside the souvenir shop.

"He did?" Selena asked, moving closer to inspect the model. Although she had been to the Alamo before, she had always given the gift shop a miss, content to soak up the tranquil atmosphere inside the shrine.

"Umm." Luke's murmur underlined his fascination with the model. "Over there—" he pointed to a section running from the mission almost to the main gate "—he had a breach closed on that side. And there—" his hand moved, his finger pointing to the inside of the Alamo itself ''—he built a dirt ramp and parapet on the east wall and mounted three cannons at the top of it. And for their prized eighteen pounder, he had a special parapet built in the southwest corner, where it had a commanding view overlooking the entire town. Brilliant.'' Luke's voice held professional admiration. ''Too bad it wasn't nearly enough.''

''But it was enough.''

His attention snagged by her soft comment, Luke turned away from the model to stare at her in puzzlement. ''What are you talking about?'' he asked, taking her by the hand and leading her from the building to the peaceful courtyard. ''The fort collapsed under Santa Anna's attack. All the defenders died.''

''I know.'' Her smile serene, Selena led him to a stone bench beneath the shading branches of an old cypress tree. ''But it was still enough, more than enough.''

''In what way? They lost.''

''The mission, yes,'' she agreed. ''But their deaths were of major significance. Those fortifications enabled the defenders to hold out for thirteen days, giving Sam Houston the precious time he needed to gather an army. And then, inspired by the rallying cry from the Alamo, that army dealt a humiliating blow of defeat to Santa Anna at San Jacinto a mere seven weeks after the Alamo fell.''

Luke was quiet for some seconds, then a crooked smile curved his lips. ''You were humoring me in there.'' He moved his head to indicate the gift shop. ''Weren't you?''

Selena's braid bounced on her shoulders as she shook her head in denial. "No. I knew the story of the Alamo," she explained. "I even knew there had been fortifications made to make the mission more defensible. But I honestly didn't know what those fortifications consisted of until you pointed them out to me." Her expression remained serene, but her voice held a taunt. "Now, tell me that you didn't know the story of how the clarion call of Remember the Alamo was the deciding factor in the crushing defeat of Santa Anna."

"Of course I knew," Luke admitted, shrugging. "But, inside there, I was referring strictly to the well-thought-out and engineered fortifications."

"And, with your architect's eye for detail," she opined in a dry tone, "you were admiring the skill of Green Jameson, the garrison engineer."

Luke arched his eyebrows in questioning surprise. "You know that I'm an architect?"

"Of course I know." Selena's shrug mirrored his. "It was one of the first things I heard about you."

His lowered eyebrows met in a frown. "One of the first? What else have you heard?"

"Not much," she confessed. "Other than that you're originally from Pennsylvania, divorced, something of a loner and that you're building a house on a piece of land you bought from Will a mile or so up-river from the place you're now renting from him—all I heard was that you have gained worldwide respect and fame for your innovative designs."

"Not much?" Luke shook his head. "I'd say that was quite a bit, and a lot more than I know about you."

"You had only to ask."

"And you would have answered?" His expression was skeptical.

"Maybe." Laughing, Selena stood and held out her hand to him. "But you won't know unless you try."

Clasping her hand, Luke rose to tower over her. "I'll keep that in mind. Where do we go from here?"

"On a short tour of the city," she replied, yanking his hand to get him moving. "Come along. If we don't hurry, we'll miss the open-air trolley bus."

"This, ladies and gentlemen, is King William, San Antonio's most famous residential neighborhood." The tour trolley driver paused in his routine to take a breath. Selena seized the moment to insert a comment.

"Since you're an architect," she murmured to Luke, indicating the imposing homes that lined the broad street, "I thought this section of town would interest you. It contains a variety of building styles."

"It does," Luke said, running an expert glance over two houses designed in the Colonial Revival style. The collection of homes and architecture was eclectic, to say the least, ranging from compact to polychromed Romanesque. "The restoration work is beautiful."

"Yes, I've always loved this—" She broke off as the guide resumed speaking.

"The period of neglect of these historical homes that began in the 1940s has been arrested and . . ."

Luke tuned the guide out, not because of boredom, but because he had other, more personal and pressing things than houses to think about.

Selena. He wanted her. Again. No, not again, Luke corrected himself, but still. The wanting was constant, and it was beginning to bother him because his desire had expanded to encompass much more than physical release.

The physical need was still there, simmering close to the surface. By itself, that was uncomfortable enough, but now there was an additional factor for him to deal with. He wanted not only to possess Selena—he wanted to know the person inside the tempting package.

Questions about her hammered inside his head, tormenting his mind as unrelentingly as his desire did his body. What made her tick? What motivated her? Why had she chosen such an unusual occupation? And, most tantalizing of all, why had she remained a virgin so long?

Shifting his weight on the hard wooden bench, Luke slanted a casual glance at Selena. She wasn't paying attention to the tour monologue, either. She was looking at him, her eyes narrowed in speculation.

What was brewing inside that beautiful head of hers? What was she thinking, feeling? Was she as interested in him, the man, as he was in her, the woman? A wave of impatience swept over him. Why in hell was he asking himself these questions? Hadn't she told him that all he had to do was ask?

"You're looking very serious," he observed. "What are you thinking about?"

"You," Selena replied.

"Oh?" Luke arched his eyebrows. "What about me?"

Selena shrugged. "Just curious."

A teasing smile tilted his lips as he paraphrased her earlier remark. "You have only to ask."

"And you'll answer?" Selena asked, shooting his skeptical response back to him.

Enjoying the play, Luke carried it out to the letter. "Maybe. But you won't know unless you try."

Selena gave him a considering look, then nodded. "Okay, here goes. What are you doing in West Texas?"

"Living," Luke said sardonically. "Just living."

"Or just existing."

"Whatever." He shrugged, but she was persistent. "Burnout?"

"Of a kind."

She frowned. "Soon after I met you, I decided you had a fierce hate-on for some unfortunate woman."

"Hate-on?" Luke grinned. "Don't you mean har—"

"Hate-on," she repeated, cutting him off. Taking a quick look around to see if they were being overheard, she lowered her voice and observed, "I don't think a crowded tour bus is the place for this discussion."

"Is there a law that says we have to stay on the bus until the end of the tour?" he asked.

Selena made a face. "Of course not."

"There's your answer."

They exited the vehicle at the next scheduled stop. Luke didn't have the vaguest idea where they were or where they were going, nor did he care. His interest was aroused even more than before by her shrewd, insightful observation. He was content to stroll by her side, waiting for her to continue her analysis of his motives. But, when she did resume speaking, Selena threw him a curve.

"I think we'll head for La Villita."

Luke stopped in his tracks. "What?"

"La Villita," she said. "It's Spanish for little town, and is the original settlement of old San Antonio."

"No kidding?" His voice was dry. "And here I thought I had left the tour guide behind on the bus."

Laughing, Selena drew him aside, out of the way of pedestrian traffic. "You did," she said, leading him to a bridge spanning the San Antonio River. "This isn't part of the tour. I have a reason for going to La Villita."

Taking his familiar stance, Luke leaned on the bridge wall and cocked an eyebrow. "And that is?"

"I need to buy a dress for Brenda and Dave's wedding," she explained.

"Ah...yes, the wedding." His tone was loaded with sarcasm. "How romantic."

"There it is!" Selena exclaimed.

Startled, Luke looked around, noting the crush of people on the River Walk and in boats. However, he didn't notice anything unusual. "There *what* is?" he asked, returning his puzzled gaze to her face.

"That hint of hate I mentioned." Her expression was tight with disapproval. "I was wrong. You don't have a hate-on for a particular woman. You hate women in general," she charged. "Don't you?"

"No, Selena," he said without hesitation. "I do not hate women."

"But you really don't like them all that much, either," she retorted. "Do you?"

Luke didn't appreciate the direction her questions were taking, but since he had given her leave to ask them, he answered candidly. "Except for a few exceptions, no, I don't like women very much. But I have reason not to."

"Right." Pushing away from the wall, Selena strode across the bridge, her back rigid, her head high.

"Selena, wait." Luke was beside her in two long strides. "You asked, I answered. Did you want me to lie to you?"

She shook her head but wouldn't look at him. "No, Luke, I didn't want you to lie."

Grasping her arm, he brought her to a stop. "So what are you mad about?"

She raised her eyes to his. The shadows within the green depths caused a pang of remorse in Luke's conscience. "I'm not mad," she denied in a tone that said she was.

"No?" Luke raised a skeptical eyebrow. "Then why are you running away from me?"

"I'm not running." Selena's chin lifted to a proud angle.

"Then where are you going?" he persisted.

"Shopping." Tossing the long braid over her shoulder with a jerk of her head, Selena took off again.

Cursing himself for ruining the sense of ease and friendship they had been sharing, Luke rammed his hands into his jeans pockets and took off after her.

Except for a few exceptions, Luke did not like women. Terrific. Not being slow on the uptake, Selena hadn't failed to notice that he hadn't mentioned any names of the exceptions—notably hers.

The sense of injury she felt was shocking and revealing. Was it possible to become so emotionally involved with a man within a few short hours? Selena slid a side-long look at Luke, felt the bottom fall out of her stomach and knew that it was not only possible, but a certainty. Her feelings were engaged and she needed her head examined.

She had squandered not only her emotions but her time and virginity on a man who, though he self-admittedly didn't like women, apparently felt no qualms about using them to satisfy his physical urges. She was a fool, Selena told herself, fighting a rush of tears to her eyes. And fools deserved everything they got—good, bad or indifferent.

An old movie title sprang into her rattled mind, forcing Selena to suppress a sob of laughter. The good, the bad, and the indifferent.

The shops in the one square block known as La Villita were packed with Fiesta revelers. Shouldering her way through the throng, Selena made for a shop she had frequented many times before, which offered custom-designed clothing. Luke dogged her heels like a sleuth closing in on a suspect. At the doorway to the shop, she turned to confront him.

"I know stuff like this bores most men," she said. "And, considering your antipathy for women, I suppose it bores you more than most. I won't mind if you wait outside."

Luke heaved a sigh. "I have no antipathy for you, Selena, and you don't bore me. I'll go in with you."

Disgusted with herself for her surge of pleasure upon hearing his response, Selena turned away from him with a muttered, "Suit yourself." Moving her shoulders in a shrug she hoped conveyed unconcern, she swung open the door.

"I always do."

The shiver that washed over her owed nothing to the coolness inside the shop and everything to the warmth of Luke's breath feathering the back of her neck. Ignoring him and his effect on her senses, Selena attempted to escape by making a beeline for a rack of dresses. Telling herself she really couldn't still detect the spicy scent of his morning after-shave, she began leafing through the dresses.

"What about this?"

Praying for deliverance, Selena turned to see what Luke was referring to. The two-piece outfit he was holding aloft by a hanger brought a soft "Oh" to her lips.

"I like it," he said, shifting his gaze from the garment to Selena. "And it might even do you justice."

As much as she hated to admit it, Selena liked the dress, too. Made of crinkly gauze in a delicate shade of pale lilac, the outfit consisted of a full, swishy skirt with a broad matching sash and a camisole-style blouse with tiny pearl buttons. Both pieces were adorned with small flowers, exquisitely hand-embroidered in jewel-tone hues of emerald, pearlized pink, amethyst, silver and gold.

"Well?" Luke asked. "What do you think?"

"It's beautiful."

He thrust the hanger into her hand. "So try it on."

Selena absolutely loved the outfit. But even if she hadn't, she'd have bought it on Luke's expression alone when she stepped from the changing room to ask his opinion.

"God!" he exclaimed in a tone of awe, sweeping a glance from the hem of the skirt at her ankles, to the deep plunge where the neckline revealed the soft swell of her breasts. "You look ripe for ravishment."

"Dream on," she drawled, inwardly despairing of the flutter of excitement his remark sent rocketing through her. Head held regally, Selena swept into the changing room. Luke's laughter joined her there.

Nevertheless, she bought the outfit, silently vowing to slug him if he made another sexist comment about her or it. After waiting in line for what seemed hours to pay for her purchase, Selena fully expected Luke to suggest that they find something else to do. Instead, he confounded her by requesting her assistance.

"Okay, I helped you with your shopping. Now you can help me with mine."

Selena didn't try to hide her surprise. "You want to buy something to wear for the wedding?"

Luke gave her a droll look. "Hardly. I want to buy souvenirs for my brother and his family."

"You have a brother?" She wasn't sure exactly why the information surprised her.

His expression turned wry. "Yes, I have a brother. And, though I realize that at this point you probably regard me as an unfeeling monster, Selena, believe it or don't, I even had a mother and father."

"Had?"

"They're both gone."

"I'm sorry."

"So am I." Luke sighed, then smiled. "So, will you help me? I need a woman's advice."

"Yes, of course. I'll help." Selena frowned. "Your brother's hard to buy for?"

Luke gave a quick shake of his head. "No, not Hank. But I'm uncertain about his wife, Laura."

"Laura's picky?"

Luke laughed. "Laura's wonderful. She's an interior decorator and she has impeccable taste. I'd hate like hell to send her something she detests but feels she must display, simply because it came as a gift from me."

Wonderful. Selena felt a spark of anger spring to life inside her. Without thinking, she gave vent to her resentment. "I take it that Laura is one of the few exceptions whom you allow yourself to like?"

Unconcerned with the crowds of people streaming around him, Luke froze and pinned Selena to the sidewalk with a drilling stare. "Yes, Laura is an exception. She's special, inside and out, and she'd die for Hank."

Selena knew the feeling. For, in a place deep inside her, which she preferred not to acknowledge, she was dying a little for Luke at that very moment. It made no sense and it wasn't very smart, but then, she had always known it wasn't smart to fall in love. And Selena was falling in love. Damn him.

"And being willing to die for your brother makes her special?" In a bid to repudiate her own unwanted feelings, she lashed out with sarcasm against those of a woman she didn't even know. "How utterly Victorian."

"Selena, I told you—"

Tired of the subject and hurting unbearably inside, Selena interrupted him impatiently. "Oh, drop it! Let's get your souvenirs and get out of here."

In the end, they had no difficulty finding a gift for Laura, or for her two grown daughters from her first marriage, her son-in-law, her young granddaughter or her and Hank's six-month-old son. It was finding something for Hank that nearly drove Selena to distraction, because Luke vetoed every one of her suggestions.

"I'm beginning to think you're a little mixed up," she grumbled after he rejected yet another of her selections. "I believe you're the one who would die for Hank."

Luke gave the idea serious consideration, then nodded in agreement. "I probably would. Hank's one of the good guys of this less-than-perfect world. He put me through college, helped set me up in business and gave me comfort when my life crashed around me. He's a true, clean-to-the-bone gentleman, and I love him—no questions asked."

Feeling deservedly put in her place, yet encouraged to learn that Luke was capable of feeling the emotion of love, Selena lowered her eyes. "I'm sorry, Luke," she whispered. "I have no right to pass judgment on you or anyone close to you. I'll keep my mouth shut from now on."

Luke treated her to his devil grin. "I'll bet."

The tension between them dissipated and, with the wave of relief clearing her mind, Selena got a brilliant idea. "Luke, I've got it!" she exclaimed.

"Is it contagious?"

She made a face at him. "I've got an idea for the perfect gift for your brother. You said Hank was one of the good guys, right?"

Luke nodded. She laughed.

"Buy him a white cowboy hat!"

It was while Luke was paying for the classic white Stetson that Selena's attention was caught by a print of a Western painting. Oblivious to everything else, she was studying the print with delight when Luke strolled up to her.

"Find something interesting?"

"Look at this, Luke." Eyes sparkling, she handed the print to him. "It looks like an artist's rendition of the Indian cave paintings at Amistad Lake."

Luke glanced at the print, then narrowed his eyes for a closer inspection. "I've heard about the wall drawings in caves around the Big Bend area," he said. "But I've never heard anything about a cave at the dam. The colors and detail of these paintings are incredible." He shot a glance at her. "Are there really paintings like these there?"

"Yes," Selena answered with authority.

"You've seen them?"

"Yes."

He shook his head in amazement. "They appear virtually untouched by time and the elements."

Selena smiled. "They are."

"They're accessible?"

She nodded. "They have been ever since the dam was built, but you can only get to the cave by boat."

"Too bad." Luke sighed, disappointed. "I would have liked to see them."

Selena thought for an instant, then made an on-the-spot decision. "I have a friend in Del Rio who owns a boat," she said quickly, before she had a chance to change her mind. "And we don't have rooms for tonight." She shot a glance at her watch. "It's 3:26 now. If we can get out of San Antonio before the worst of the rush-hour craziness, we could be in Del Rio by eight o'clock or thereabout. Want to go?"

"Can we find a place to stay?"

Selena laughed. "I wouldn't think there'd be any problem. They're not having fiesta in Del Rio. And there are several very nice motels, one very close to the lake. Besides, I could call and find out."

Clasping her by the elbow, Luke began walking. "Let's find a phone."

Less than thirty minutes later, they were on their way, Selena in the lead, Luke following close behind her. After making the call to the motel, she had told Luke simply that she'd made a reservation. What she hadn't told him was that she had booked separate rooms for them.

Luke wasn't going to be overjoyed when he learned about their sleeping arrangements—Selena was certain of that. But then, she wasn't exactly thrilled over being thought of as a mere convenience for any man—especially the one she had been stupid enough to fall in love with.

She glanced at the rearview mirror and frowned. Luke's Jeep was visible a safe distance behind her.

He was going to have a fit, Selena thought, a small, defiant smile curving her lips. If he protested, she might have to teach the devil some manners.

Nine

The weather was fine for boating. The sun was bright and hot, and a light breeze ruffled the lake waters into frothy whitecaps. The cabin cruiser cleaved a path through the waves, spewing sprays of tiny droplets into the air, where they glittered with crystallike rainbow hues in the sunlight.

Luke was immune to the tranquil beauty of the scene. He was in a foul mood that was a by-product of searing frustration and simmering anger. He had spent the night in a strange bed, alone, cursing his own careless mouth and his penchant for bluntness.

Separate rooms, for God's sake! Luke's senses and his masculine ego were still reverberating from the shock he'd received when he and Selena arrived in Del Rio.

Because they had stopped for dinner along the way, it had been after nine-thirty when they pulled into the motel. Nevertheless, the pleasant young woman behind the registration desk confirmed their reservation and said that their rooms were ready for them.

Rooms—plural, as in two located in opposite wings of the building.

Luke had been hard put to contain his confusion and anger until he had the opportunity to talk to Selena in private. Smoldering in silence, he had escorted her to her room and then, after telling himself he'd be calm and reasonable, he'd exploded like a rocket on Chinese New Year.

"What is this?" he'd demanded, stepping in front of the door to bar her way into the room. "Are you still nursing a grudge because I told you I don't like most females?"

"No, Luke, I'm not nursing a grudge," Selena said, meeting his angry stare. "You're free to like or dislike whomever you please." Her chin rose a fraction. "The same as I'm free to sleep where and with whom I please."

"But—dammit! You haven't slept with anyone but me."

"Yet," she retaliated, successfully exacerbating his already fiery temper.

But, as always, when he had reached flash point, Luke didn't blaze. He turned cold, his voice chilling. "I'm warning you, Selena, if you so much as consider taking another man into your bed and body, I'll—"

"You'll what?" she'd cut him off in a tone every bit as icy as his. Raising her hands, she'd grasped his head to draw his face down to hers. "Let me tell you something, Mr. Women-are-beneath-me Branson. Until last night, I believed there wasn't a man alive worthy of the gift of my body." He could feel the breath shudder through her as she inhaled sharply. "And now, since last night, I'm convinced of it. But if and when I ever decide to bestow that gift again, *I'll* decide with whom I'll share it. And there's not a damned thing you can do about it, and you know it."

Luke opened his mouth to argue...plead...beg. But Selena kept him silent in the most effective way imaginable. Tugging him closer, she covered his mouth with her own. Hope and anticipation sprang to riotous life inside him. It died an agonizing death when she released him and stepped back.

"Sleep on that, *lover*." Her voice was flat, devoid of feeling. "Because that's all you're going to get from me. Now—" her tone grew a hard edge "—I'd appreciate it if you'd get the hell out of my way. I'm tired."

Luke did as she ordered, not from intimidation, but simply because she suddenly did look tired—more than tired. All at once, Selena looked exhausted and on the point of shattering. And Luke wasn't certain he could bear being the cause of her collapse.

Feeling an odd sense of alarm and a stirring emotion he refused to recognize or contemplate, Luke had gone to his room. Alone and aching through the night, he had buried the unwanted feelings sprouting inside beneath a smothering layer of frustration and anger.

"You okay, buddy?"

The call came from behind him, from Selena's friend, Dan, who was seated in the shaded pilot's chair beneath the protective covering of the boat's canopy. Selena was ensconced in the chair opposite her friend.

"Yeah, fine," Luke shouted over the noise of the powerful outboard engine. "Thanks, *buddy*," he muttered in a growl under his breath.

Luke rested his head against the leather-padded divider between the pilot's seat and the rest of the boat, and took a swig from the icy can he was clutching.

"How's your beer holding out?" Dan yelled. "Ready for another?"

Since it wasn't yet noon and he was working on his second beer, Luke was about to decline the offer. Then he thought, Why the hell not? Maybe the brew would dull the ache clawing at his loins and the self-directed anger tearing at his emotions.

"Sure, I'll have another," he called back, tilting the can he held to his lips and draining it in two long swallows.

Selena brought the fresh can to him . . . along with a frown of disapproval. "You're going to get plastered," she said, slapping the new can into his hand.

Luke stared at her from beneath the wide brim of the straw hat Dan had given him to wear. "Bag it, Green Eyes," he snarled. "In case you hadn't noticed, I'm a man, not a boy. I don't need a prissy, late-to-the-gate, oversensitive snip of a woman telling me what to do." Luke regretted his spate the instant it was out of his mouth, and even more so as he watched a vulnerable, injured expression darken her beautiful eyes. Her breath made a hissing sound as she gasped.

Then the hurt look was gone, replaced by a glittering sheen of fury.

"Prissy! Oversensitive! You—you egoistical jerk!" Her voice was pitched just high enough to reach him over the roar of the engine.

"Look, Selena, I'm sorry. I didn't sleep well." Luke offered her a wry, self-deprecating smile. Her exquisite breasts rose and fell in time with her breathing, making his hands burn and itch with the need to touch, caress, stroke their silky fullness. "I was lonely, sleeping alone. I missed having you curled up next to me, needing me, warming me." The admission hadn't been easy for him to make, but she dismissed his discomfort with an angry toss of her head.

"You're not sorry, you're horny," she said in scathing tones. "Well, I've got a news bulletin for you, bucko. I don't particularly care if you drink yourself into the middle of next month. Because after we've seen the cave and are off this lake, I'll be long gone." She leaned close to his face to ensure that he heard every one of her caustic words. "And I don't give a damn if you have to sleep alone forever. Because, *Dark Eyes*, you've earned your solitude."

Luke didn't watch her walk away from him—he couldn't. If he had, he wouldn't have been able to stop himself from grabbing her, holding her, kissing her until, senseless, she surrendered herself, body and soul, into his possession.

His expression taut, he stared into the vastness of the lake and raised the can to his mouth. The tremor in his fingers caught his attention. Frowning, he set the can of beer aside untouched, thinking that all the beer in the world wouldn't solve his problems.

Selena slid onto the chair and stared through the windshield. She couldn't look back, wouldn't look back at him. She couldn't stand seeing him like this, so cold and bitter, withdrawn and sarcastic. What had become of the laughing man with whom she had made such joyous, glorious love?

Did that laughing man really exist, other than in her own beguiled imagination? Probably not, Selena reflected, recalling the aloof, sardonic, handsome devil of a man Will had introduced to her as Luke Branson.

Luke.

Selena swallowed a sigh of regret for the man he might have been and blinked against the sting of tears in her eyes. Why had she gone and done such a damn fool thing as fall in love with him? she berated herself. She hadn't suffered the panic of sensing time running out on her biological clock. She hadn't even felt the pressing need to fulfill herself as a woman. So why—*what* was the attraction?

He was the strong, silent type. The phrase whispered through her mind. A tear escaped her eye, and Selena brushed it away with an impatient flick of her trembling fingers. Luke was strong and silent, and she had proved herself a pushover.

It was enough to depress Pollyanna.

"Coming up on the cave."

Dan's cheery voice drew Selena from her fruitless self-examination. There would be time—years and empty years of nothing but time—to brood about her lapse of common sense. But for now, it was time to put on a bright face for Dan, if only to keep her old friend from the realization that she and Luke were now enemies.

Selena slid off the chair as Dan steered the craft alongside a narrow pier. "I'll secure," she offered, making her way to the rear of the boat. Looking none too steady on his feet, Luke was standing on the dock side of the boat. "I said, I'll secure," she shouted, just as the boat bumped against the pier.

Luke either didn't hear her or didn't want to. Without acknowledging her call, he leaped over the side, stumbled, then turned to catch the line she tossed to him. After securing the boat, he held out his hand to assist her. Ignoring his hand, Selena stepped with practiced ease onto the gently swaying pier.

"You should have let me do it," she said, glaring at him. "You almost took a header into the lake."

"I did not," Luke retorted, obviously annoyed by her assessment of his condition. "But, even if I had, I'd have been all right," he went on in a taunting tone. "The expert river guide would have rescued me."

"Don't bank on it," Selena snapped. Turning away from him, she strode to the end of the pier, where it butted against a rock-strewn bank. "We have to climb this incline to get to the cave," she told him when he came up behind her. She swung around to give him a doubtful look. "Think you can make it?"

"Dammit, Selena, I am not—" he began, but she cut him off with a soft command.

"Keep your voice down. I don't want Dan to hear us."

Reminded of their host, Luke shot a look at the boat. "Where is Dan? Isn't he coming with us?"

"No." Shaking her head, Selena turned and stepped onto the bank. "He's preparing lunch in the galley." With the agility of a veteran climber, she scrambled up the incline.

Grunting and cursing, Luke was right behind her. "Why didn't you tell me about this bank?" he grumbled. "I'd have worn my climbing boots."

Stepping onto the narrow footpath, Selena paused to slant a bored look at him. "That little slope could hardly be referred to as a climb," she said over her shoulder. "Little old ladies and small children do it without difficulty."

"Not in heeled cowboy boots," Luke muttered, trailing her along the path.

Selena came to a stop at the end of a chain-link fence, which stretched across the opening of a shallow cave. "You wanted to see the paintings," she said, motioning to the area beyond the fence. "There they are. Quit grousing and look at them."

Closing the distance between them, Luke came to stand beside her in front of the fence. He peered into the cave and frowned. "I don't see anything."

"Keep looking," she said. "You'll see them when your eyes adjust to the dimness inside. The lack of direct light is one of the reasons the paintings are still so vivid."

Luke was quiet for a moment, face pressed to the fence. Then he exclaimed in quiet awe, "I see them! Selena, they're fantastic!"

Selena felt emotion stir inside her. Against her will, she found herself sharing his wonder and excitement. "Yes, they are. Tell me what you see."

He answered without looking at her. "At the end of the cave, as if it were standing guard, there's a huge cat—a mountain lion or leopard—painted blue. There are other animals—deer or antelope—and a bunch of symbols I can't decipher." He moved along the fence as he spoke, unmindful of the rocky, uneven ground. "I see what appears to be an elongated figure in flowing robes and a domelike structure. And...son of a gun!" he exclaimed as he reached the far end of the cave. "Selena, there's another large cat at this end!"

"Yes." Selena had paced in silence behind him, seeing it all fresh through his eyes. "Did you notice that both the cats face away from the cave?"

"Yes, of course," Luke nodded. "It's like they were put there to protect the mural between them."

"That's what I thought the first time I saw it."

"This is great." Luke spared a quick glance at her. "Do you have any idea how old they are?"

Selena shrugged. "I've been told that they have been dated to somewhere around two thousand years ago."

"Incredible."

"Yes, I—" Selena broke off as Dan's voice rose to them from the lake.

"Lunch is ready whenever you two are."

"Coming!" Selena called, then turned to retrace their steps along the fence. Luke followed at a slower pace, his gaze riveted to the cave wall.

Picking his way, Luke descended the bank almost as nimbly as Selena. "We've got company," he said leaping onto the pier next to her. He jerked his head to indicate another boat approaching.

"Hum," Selena murmured, nodding. "Looks like we'll have to postpone lunch until Dan locates another place to dock."

Dan confirmed her opinion when they drew alongside the boat. "We're going to move out and let them come in," he said, indicating the newcomers. "If you'll cast off, I'll go rev the engine."

"Right." Selena moved to the line securing the bow, and Luke turned to the one at the stern.

Instead of standing off, the newcomer kept circling, creating waves that set Dan's boat rocking. It alternately banged into the pier, then moved away from it. Selena freed the bowline, then, her timing perfect, leaped onto the boat. Luke's timing wasn't as accurate. He freed the line and leaped without pause as the boat danced away from the pier.

Luke dropped like a stone into the churning lake.

Selena didn't think, she reacted. Responding to training and conditioning—and to selfless love—she sprinted to the rear of the craft and dove into the icy water after him.

The scene that ensued might have been funny if Selena hadn't been so scared...and Luke hadn't been so angry. Sputtering and cursing, he fought her attempt to help him.

"Dammit, I'm all right!" he shouted, pushing her away. "I don't need rescuing, you bimbo! I can swim." Proving his point, he struck out for the side of the boat, where Dan was waiting to hoist him aboard.

"Fine!" Selena shouted after him. "If nothing else, maybe the dunking in this cold water will sober you up!" Ignoring the hand Luke reached down to her, she grasped Dan's hand and scrambled into the boat.

"I didn't need sobering, damn you!" Luke attacked the minute she was safely on board. "I wasn't drunk."

"Says you," Selena retaliated in a sneering voice. "And, for your information, the word *bimbo* is masculine by definition. Look that up in your dictionary."

They didn't stop for lunch. Soaking wet and fuming in chilling silence, they picked at the food during the run back to the marina.

Her emotions as churned-up as the lake waters had been, Selena sat staring through the windshield. She felt sorry for Dan who, by the puzzled glances he shifted from her to Luke, didn't understand what was going on. But, sorry for him or not, she didn't feel inclined toward enlightening her friend. Maybe someday she would—if she lived to be about a hundred years old.

The return trip seemed to take forever. Her feelings raw, Selena gnawed on her lips and wished it was over. All she wanted was to get away from Luke, as fast and as far as possible.

Once again, she felt embarrassed and humiliated by a man. The fact that she happened to be in love with this particular man didn't alleviate the sense of depression blanketing her mind. Instead, it magnified it.

The combination of the hot afternoon sun and the stiff breeze created by the forward thrust of the boat dried Selena and Luke's clothing. In a rush to get away, Selena helped Dan secure the boat. Then, with a quick hug and a whispered apology, she headed for her car.

"Selena, wait!" Luke called, loping after her. He caught up to her as she was unlocking her car. "Are you going back to the motel?"

Shaking her head, she slipped behind the steering wheel. "I'm going home."

"But that's a long drive and it's already almost dinnertime," he protested. "Why not wait until morning? I—I think we should talk."

Selena shook from the battle waging inside her. She wanted to stay with him, longed to be with him, yet knew it would destroy her if he hurt her again. Her pride was stiff. "No, Luke. We have nothing to talk about." She fired the engine and the car sprang to life with a growl. "I'm going home, and I'd appreciate it if you'd stay out of my way from now on." Fighting tears, she set the car into motion. The tires spewed a cloud of dust and gravel as she tore away from the parking area.

An unfamiliar feeling of desolation permeated Luke's being. He stood as if turned to stone, watching Selena's car growing smaller in the distance.

"What's with you two?" Dan asked, coming to stand alongside him.

"The lady doesn't like me," Luke replied, turning to give the other man a wry smile.

Dan snorted. "Like hell!"

Luke frowned. "What do you mean?"

"Look, buddy, I've known that lady a long time," Dan said, jerking his thumb in the direction of Selena's disappearing car. "And I've never seen her look at a man the way she looks at you. It was as clear as daylight."

"What was?" Luke asked, hoping—yet afraid to hope.

Dan grinned. "Buddy, that lady is so much in love with you that it shines like a beacon from her eyes."

Love.

The word occupied Luke's mind throughout every one of the long miles from Del Rio to Study Butte.

Was it possible? he asked himself, not once but several times before and after leaving Dan with heartfelt thanks. Could Selena have fallen in love with him so quickly? Or was whatever Dan saw shining from her eyes the delayed aftermath of lovemaking? The latter seemed more likely, if a lot more unacceptable to Luke.

But why unacceptable? He delved into his own somewhat murky emotions. The last thing he wanted in his life was love. Wasn't it? Until he'd met a cat-witch woman with green eyes and black hair, Luke had been convinced that he would never again fall into the emotion-mangling trap.

Love turned sour was a killer of all softening, humanizing emotions. And love invariably went sour, Luke assured himself.

But did it? The question whispered inside Luke's head, bringing a frown to his granite features. Weren't there individual instances of love that deepened and grew stronger over time, rather than deteriorating?

Luke wasn't forced to rake his mind for examples of that particular theory. He had personally witnessed strong bonds of love as recently as a few days ago.

His memory flashed a collage—scenes of three long-married couples laughing and enjoying life and each other. They had gotten wet, too, but they had relished the fun, not argued about it.

What had that man said? Wasn't it something about wringing every ounce of pleasure from life? Yes, that was it, Luke recalled. And, at the time, he had shrugged and muttered, "Whatever works."

But nothing had worked in any meaningful way for Luke in a long time—too long a time. He had been deeply hurt by his wife's defection and the subsequent loss of his rights to his daughter. And, because of the depth of his pain, Luke knew he had withdrawn into himself, erecting a protective facade of bitterness and arrogance.

Night was falling, but light was dawning inside Luke. With new insight, he realized that what he had so arrogantly dismissed as middle-aged boredom was in fact loving sharing between three couples who genuinely enjoyed themselves and each other. He had thought that by vacationing together, they no longer desired privacy to be together. He had conveniently forgotten that all they had to do was shut the doors to their rooms to have all the privacy they desired.

Shaking his head in disbelief over his own lack of perception, Luke drove the Jeep onto the driveway of the house he rented from Will, then sat staring at the star-studded sky. Selena had called him a jerk, among other things. A derisive smile tilted his tight lips. She was right. She just hadn't gone far enough, he thought wryly. He wasn't a jerk, or even a bimbo. In his own late-to-the-gate, newly-enlightened opinion, Luke decided he was an absolute jackass.

Did jackasses deserve a second chance? The question kept Luke awake and once again pacing the patio throughout what was left of the night.

Selena had ordered him to stay out of her way, and when she'd said it, she had sounded like she meant it. But did she? Luke knew he had hurt her by not making her an exception when he'd admitted to not liking women.

Spearing his fingers through his hair, Luke circled the patio and strode into the house. Would Selena understand, and perhaps forgive him, if he explained to her why he felt as he did? More importantly, would she even talk to him?

Watching predawn change the darkness into luminescent pearl gray, Luke felt the last barrier crumble and collapse inside him. He had to make her listen to him, had to make her understand and forgive him. For, like it or not—and amazingly, he did like it— Luke knew he was irrevocably in love with Selena.

One memory held out hope for Luke. He heard the echo of his own voice telling Selena that Laura would die for his brother, Hank. Luke clung to the image of

Selena plunging into the lake to save him without pausing to consider herself.

He prayed that his memory and Dan's observation were both correct.

Ten

The incessant ringing of the phone woke Selena in midafternoon. Although she possessed not an ounce of psychic ability, she knew who was on the other end of the line. Luke had rung her phone at least half a dozen times since first light. She had answered three times. On the third call, she told him succinctly that she had nothing to say to him and asked him politely not to call again. Luke's response had been to tell her that he would keep ringing until she agreed to talk to him. She retaliated by not answering the phone after that.

But Selena was fully awake now and getting madder by the second. Muttering expletives, she reached out and yanked the cord from the wall jack.

Anger sustained her while she showered and dressed. Its impetus waned as she sipped her first cup of coffee. Her eyes haunted, she stared at the kitchen wall phone.

Maybe she should... No! Selena aborted the traitorous thought. She would not give in to her need to see Luke and talk to him one more time. It was over. Done. Finished. And, unless she kept herself busy and moving and away from him, it might very likely be the finish of her, as well.

Acting on that speculation, Selena scraped back her chair and stood up. Busy and moving. That was the answer. Cradling her cup, she returned to her bedroom, connected the phone jack and quickly punched in the number of the tour office, silently praying Luke wouldn't be there. Relief trembled through her at the familiar sound of Will's rough voice.

"It's Selena, Will," she said, amazed at the carefree tone she managed to produce.

"Oh, back again, are you?" Will growled.

"Back and bored." Selena laughed, then winced at the harsh sound of her voice. "I need something to do." At least that was the truth. "Got something for me?"

"Only about three different jobs," Will retorted. "You can take your pick."

"Run them by me."

"I've got a half-day float, a full-day backroads tour and an overnight Santa Elena trip, all for tomorrow morning," he said. "Which one do you want?"

Knowing the Santa Elena trip was for two to four days, Selena didn't hesitate. "I'll take the overnight. How big is the party, and which trip did they choose?"

Will answered with his usual economy of words. "One raft, party of six. You'll be on your lonesome."

An odd note in his tone alerted Selena. Frowning, she asked, "So what? Is there a problem?"

"I hope not," he replied. "But, well, there's been a report of some shooting in that area."

"Shooting!" Selena exclaimed. "Was anybody injured?"

"No, no," Will assured her. "The narcotic agents think there may be some fighting among the drug runners."

Selena sighed. "That's a relief. For a minute there, I thought you meant that someone was shooting at our people."

"No," Will repeated in a soothing tone. "I feel sure this was just an isolated incident, but I thought it only fair to tell you about it."

"Okay, Will, thanks." Selena's jangling nerves calmed down enough to let her concentrate on business. "Is this a mixed group you've got for me?"

Will's gravelly laughter sang along the wire. "All females." His laughter ended on a snort. "They're all writers. Said they want to do the tour for research purposes."

The information snagged Selena's interest. "Writers? What kind, journalists?"

"Nah." Will snorted. "Fiction writers. Historical." His tone took on an edge of ridicule. "Or was it hysterical?"

Chauvinist. Keeping her opinion to herself, Selena replied, "I sincerely hope not."

"And I sincerely believe you're in for one dandy of a trip," Will drawled. "Wanna change your mind?"

"Nope," she answered at once. "I'll come down to the warehouse in a little while to check out the gear." Deciding she'd check in with her friend while she was at it, Selena went on, "By the way, is Brenda working this afternoon?"

"No," Will replied. "Dave took a group on a ten-day trip to the lower canyons. Brenda went along for the ride."

Lucky, plucky Brenda, Selena thought, smiling at the idea of her flighty friend roughing it with her lover. "I was away only two days, " she mused aloud. "When did they leave?"

"Yesterday morning," Will said. "A group wanted to take the tour. Dave offered to do it, and our impetuous Brenda opted to go along with him."

"Yep, that's our Brenda." Selena laughed. "Okay, Will, I'll stop in at the office after I've checked the gear."

Three hours later, Selena walked into the office and had to fight the urge to turn in her tracks and walk out again. Looking like every maiden's prayer for a strong, silent someone, Luke was propped against the counter in his now-familiar nonchalant pose. His jeans were tight and faded. His shirt had seen better days.

His boots were scarred and scruffy. To Selena, he looked wonderful.

"There's something wrong with your phone," he said tersely, without preamble.

Eyeing him warily, Selena stood by the door, just in case she needed to make a quick getaway. "No, there isn't," she replied, her expression daring him to refute her.

He accepted. "Must be. I was trying to call you all day and all I got was a busy signal."

Her sweet smile was taunting. "I didn't want to be disturbed, so I took the phone off the hook."

Her tone didn't faze him. "Won't do you any good," he said, with annoying confidence. "You'll have to agree to talk to me sooner or later."

"Indeed?" She arched her eyebrows.

"Sure." He nodded. "Because I won't quit until you do." Pushing away from the counter, he took a step toward her. She inched toward the door. "Selena." Luke's voice was raw. Heaving a sigh, he backed up. "Okay, I won't crowd you. But will you let me say just one thing?"

"Make it quick," she ordered. "I'm in a hurry." It wasn't a lie. She felt a sudden urgency to flee, to run away from him—before she gave in to a yearning to run into his arms.

He wet his lips. She stifled a groan. "Look, Green Eyes, this conflict between us is unnecessary. If you'd just listen to me, let me explain, we could put an end to it."

"I *did* end it—yesterday," she reminded him.

His patience snapped. "Dammit, I meant the mis-understanding between us, and you know it." He paused to draw a harsh breath, then continued more calmly, "It's not over, Selena, and you know that as well as I do. What we shared was good, too good to toss aside without so much as talking about it."

What he said made sense. Selena frowned. Why did he have to make sense? She didn't want to listen sim-ply because she was afraid he'd sweet-talk her into believing anything he wanted her to believe. But, then again, she ached for him so much. . . .

"Selena?" There was a hint of hope in his voice. She was weakening, and he knew it. "Please?"

She gave in with a soft sigh. "All right, I'll listen."

Luke's sigh was louder. "Not here," he said. "We need to talk in private. Tonight? Your place?"

She shook her head. "No, not tonight, Luke. I'm tired." A chiding smiled curved her lips. "I didn't sleep well last night. Someone kept ringing my phone."

He didn't appear at all repentant. "Maybe you should have answered. This strain and distance be-tween us might be history if you had."

His comment jogged her memory. "That reminds me, you'll have to wait a few days for a meeting, pri-vate or otherwise."

"Why do we have to wait a few days?" he asked, puzzled.

"I have a three-day float to Santa Elena," she ex-plained. "It's a party of six, all historical-fiction writers."

Luke was less than pleased. He scowled. "Can't you get out of it, let one of the others do it?"

Selena was shaking her head before he'd finished speaking. "No, Will's shorthanded. I agreed to do it, and I'll do it." She frowned. "Where is Will, anyway?"

"He had an errand to run. He told me you'd be stopping in." A tantalizing smile twitched the corners of his lips. "I told him I'd be happy to wait here for you."

He was getting to her. The liquefying process had commenced inside her. Fighting the feeling—and him—she gave him a droll look. "You're all heart, Branson."

"Not quite," he murmured in a sexy drawl. "But I'll wait till we're alone to show you."

That did it. Grasping the doorknob, Selena yanked open the door and gulped for fresh air. "I've got to go," she said, stepping backward over the threshold. "I'll see you . . . ah, talk to you, when I get back from Santa Elena."

"I can't wait," Luke called softly after her.

Damn you, you devil, Selena thought dashing for her car. She couldn't wait, either.

The sun was a brazen disk in a cobalt-blue sky. The air was dry, the river placid, and the passengers animated and noisy. Though working to move the raft along, Selena was enjoying every minute of it.

To her relief and delight, the women writers were not only pleasant, but intelligent, witty and determined to make the most of their research trip. They plied Selena with questions and listened attentively to her answers. Two of them even jotted down notes to refresh their memories later.

By midafternoon, the temperature was in the nineties, but the women didn't complain. They laughed as one woman in her forties declared that a good sweat would not only clean their facial pores but melt some of the lard clinging to their hips, as well.

They were bantering away, Selena laughing with them, when the first rifle shot rang out. Exclamations erupted from each of the women.

"What in hell was that!"

"That wasn't a shot . . . I hope!"

"Damn, that sounded like a shot to me!"

Another shot rang out, silencing the chatter. Selena gasped in disbelief as she felt the bullet whiz past her head. "Good God!" she cried. "That shot was aimed at us!" Springing into action, she applied her strength to the oars, heading for the American side of the river, opposite from where the shots had come.

"Can we do anything to help?" the youngest member of the group asked, wide-eyed.

"Yes," Selena grunted, pulling on the oars. "The instant the raft touches shore, dive for cover behind those rocks." She jerked her head to indicate a jumble of huge boulders close to the bank.

Without wasting breath on screams, or even whimpers the women scrambled from the craft the instant it scraped the sandy shoreline. Selena was right behind them. Panting, they dashed for the protective cover of the rocks. A bullet chipped a piece from a boulder as Selena followed the last woman around it.

The oldest group member, a woman in her mid fifties, swore angrily as she grabbed Selena's arm and yanked her to safety. "That clown across the river is one sick character."

Selena said, "That clown over there is probably one sick drug runner."

The startlingly pretty woman in the group groaned. "Larry didn't want me to come on this trip. Now I'll probably have to spend the rest of my life listening to him chant 'I told you so, I told you so.' "

Selena couldn't help herself, she had to laugh at the woman's menacing voice and the other women joined in. Their laughter was abruptly terminated by a bullet zinging overhead.

"Oh, Lord, what'll we do?" One woman asked the question, and all of them looked at Selena.

"We stay put," she answered. "He's got us pinned down here, but he can't shoot through rock."

"But what if he decides to cross the river?"

Sliding to the ground to sit with her back against the boulder, Selena closed her eyes. "Then, ladies, I'm afraid we'll be in some serious trouble."

Luke had deserted his post at the counter. He was seated in his employer's chair, booted feet propped on Will's paper-strewn desk. He was bored. He was restless. And he was missing Selena something fierce. The sound of tires screeching to a stop in front of the office drew his eyes to the door. An instant later, Jasper Chance barged into the room.

"Raphael just ran into the store to tell me that some drug-running bastard has Selena and her party trapped in the rocks downriver."

The desk chair tumbled backward as Luke sprang to his feet.

"What do you mean, trapped?" he demanded.

"The guy's firing on them with a 30-30," Jasper said, and turned the air blue with a string of curses.

Luke froze for an instant. Then he started for the door, his veins flowing with ice. "Can you loan me a gun?" he asked Jasper, pausing beside him. Jasper responded with a sharp nod.

"Where are you going, Luke?" Will called as Luke strode through the doorway.

"Hunting," Luke said without looking back.

Jasper was right behind him. "I own two guns, I'll go with you."

Luke and Jasper crossed the river a few miles from the tour office. Jasper's friend Raphael provided horses for them, along with directions to where the sniper was located. Luke hadn't been on horseback for years. Yet, after settling into the saddle, he handled the animal like an expert.

"Gracias, amigo," Luke murmured, kneeing the horse to get him moving. He didn't hear Raphael's response.

There wasn't one man across the river from the boulders, there were three. Following the echo of the rifle reports, Luke and Jasper galloped as close to the area as they could without being heard, then walked their horses even closer. Dismounting, they agreed in whispers to circle around the three men and close in from opposite directions.

But they weren't the first rescuers on the scene. There were four narcotics agents, all sharpshooters, positioning themselves for clear shots. Luke, following an unfamiliar desire to destroy another human being, moved in too close. He drew the drug runners' fire, which revealed their cover. The narcotics agents shot back, and their aim was better. Within minutes, it was all over but the shouting—and some loud yells from a drug runner who had taken a bullet in the leg.

Leaving the snipers in the agents' capable hands, Luke and Jasper remounted and swam their horses across the river. Fear rode tandem with Luke.

"Selena!" he called, as his horse clambered onto the narrow sandy bank.

"Luke!" Selena cried, darting around a boulder. "Oh, God! Are you trying to get yourself killed? There's a man with a rifle over there!" Unmindful of her own safety, she ran down the bank, flinging herself into his arms as he dismounted.

Shutting his eyes, Luke crushed her precious body against his thundering heart. "Are you all right?" Pushing her away, he skimmed a wild-eyed look over her trembling body. "You weren't hit, wounded?"

"No." Gasping calming breaths, Selena shook her head. "I'm fine and, thank God, so are my ladies." She turned to smile at the women, who were slowly emerging from behind the rocks.

"You ladies okay?" Jasper called.

A chorus of yesses rang out, accompanied by a dry retort from the oldest woman, "That little incident did my heart good. The old ticker hasn't beat so hard and fast with excitement since the last time I had sex.''

The laughter the remark generated was needed, and it was appreciated by Selena, who now faced getting the women back to the tour office. But when she announced her decision to abort the trip, it was met by an outcry of protests.

"You can't continue," Luke said, sweeping the group with a stern expression. His declaration was received with coolly voiced ridicule.

"You think not?"

"Wanna bet?"

"On whose authority?"

"Watch us!"

Outnumbered, Luke looked at Selena. Agreeing with the ladies, Selena grinned.

"There's your answer," she said, shrugging off his frown. "I'll see you when I get back."

"I'll be waiting." Luke repeated his statement of the day before, then added, "At my place."

The rest of the trip went off without a hitch. To Selena's pleasant surprise, the women were even more animated than before, and proved to be interesting and, at times, hilarious companions. When the trip was over and they were back at the tour office, they told a relieved Will that they had gathered enough research for several books. Then they made Selena promise to read them and provided publication dates for her.

Smiling, Selena waved them off before jumping back on the bus to return to the warehouse to stow the gear. When the job was completed, she stood staring into space, irresolute and uncertain.

For over two days, she had refused to speculate on her meeting with Luke. Now the time had come. He had risked his life for her. To Selena's knowledge, Luke didn't own a gun of his own. She didn't know if he even knew how to use one. Yet he had managed to get a rifle and ride to her defense. His action said more about his feelings for her than his words ever could.

He loved her. Selena knew it as surely as she knew that she loved him. But did Luke know it? Perhaps it was time for her to find out. Exhaling, she squared her shoulders and walked to her car. She'd go to his place, as he had asked—no, ordered—her to do. But first, she needed a shower.

Selena was clean and fresh, her loose hair gleaming with shampooed highlights when she parked her car in Luke's driveway. Lights blazed from the windows, though there was no sign of Luke.

Selena stepped from her car nervous, excited and dreading that he'd deny his love, but offer his body in return for the use of hers. The haunting strains of Tchaikovsky's first piano concerto floated on the evening breeze, wrapping Selena within their sweeping folds. She groaned and closed her eyes.

She could have handled Handel.

But Tchaikovsky? She was lost. Like a sleepwalker, Selena followed the music along the side of the house, onto the patio, then through the open doors into the living room. Luke was reclining on a club chair, head back, his eyes closed. She didn't make a sound and yet, somehow he knew she was there. He opened his eyes and stood up. He didn't say a word, but she felt him calling to her. She walked toward him. He held out his arms. Feeling like she was going home, Selena walked into his embrace and raised her mouth for his kiss.

"I missed you." His words were a whisper against her mouth.

"I missed you, too," she murmured.

"I want you."

"I want you more."

Lifting his head, Luke stared into her glowing eyes. His smile was warm and loving, and sexy as the devil. "We can talk, later," he said, nibbling on her bottom lip.

"If we must," she replied, sighing.

"I have explanations I need to give to you."

"I'll listen."

Luke exhaled in relief. "There are questions I have to ask you."

"I'll answer them," she promised.

"One thing," he murmured, pulling back to look at her.

She sighed again. "Will you cut to the chase?"

"I love you." Luke held his breath.

Selena smiled. "I love you more."

Laughing, Luke swept her into his arms. "We'll see about that." Cradling her close, he strode to the bedroom.

Epilogue

"**I** think he resembles our side of the family, Luke." Hank Branson made the observation, peering into the solemn face of his nephew who, along with his parents, was making a belated Christmas visit to the Branson's home in Pennsylvania.

"Resembles?" Laughing, Hank's wife, Laura, stared at the infant in her arms. "He looks exactly like Luke."

"Yeah." Luke's voice was rich with smug satisfaction. "He's a handsome little devil."

"Really?" Selena gave her husband an innocent, thus suspicious look. "I think he looks more like a tiny, wrinkled, grouchy old man. But if you insist that Chase looks like you—well . . ." She shrugged as her voice faded.

Luke worked at a scowl, but lost the effort in the laughter ringing through the room. In less than a year, he had lost the knack for effective scowling—a loss that was all due to Selena's love.

Absorbing the atmosphere of contentment in his brother's home, Luke gazed at his wife with eyes glowing from inner happiness. Selena was his everything. The advent of their son, born the month before on Christmas morning, expanded the boundaries of Luke's everything.

Luke adored his son, though in truth, he had been hoping for a daughter. He missed his firstborn and knew he would always miss her, but Luke had not wished for a girl to replace the daughter he had lost. No, Luke had hoped for a daughter simply because he thrilled at the idea of a reproduction of Selena.

"Luke." Selena's whisper interrupted his introspection, and the melting softness in her eyes drew him to her side.

"Hey, Laura and I would be delighted to baby-sit if you two want to go to your room and be alone for a while," Hank offered with a suggestive, understanding grin.

A faint flush of embarrassment invaded Selena's cheeks. Unperturbed by his brother's teasing, Luke returned the grin, along with a dry retort. "It's close enough to bedtime—I can contain my itch until the house is quiet and Chase is settled for the night." He arched one winged eyebrow. "But, since your little one is already settled for the night, Selena and I will excuse the two of you."

Laura sighed and sent Selena a woman-to-woman look. "Do they ever think of anything other than sex?"

In turn, Selena gave the question due consideration before replying. "Luke occasionally thinks about food."

Luke wasn't offended, he was amused... and reminded. "Now that you mention it, I'm hungry."

"Yeah," Hank seconded, laughing at his wife's long-suffering expression. "How about a snack, honey?"

"Yeah," Laura echoed in a wry tone. "How about that. It must be all of two and a half hours since dinner." She glanced at Selena as she placed the baby into Hank's competent care. "Want to help me rustle up something to eat for these two starving males?"

Selena heaved an exaggerated sigh. "I suppose I'd better. Luke gets *sooo* cranky when he's hungry." She gave him a sweet smile in passing. He retaliated by grabbing her and planting a swift, hard kiss on her surprised lips. Flustered but laughing, she followed Laura into the kitchen.

Hank's shrewd eyes didn't miss a nuance of the scene. "You know," he murmured, "I haven't seen you looking this happy in years, Luke."

"I haven't felt this happy in..." Luke's voice trailed away then. Grinning, he went on, "I've never felt this happy."

"The bitterness is gone?"

Luke's nod was decisive. "Yes."

"Good." Hank sighed his relief. "Now, I have one other question to ask."

"And that is?"

"Where did you and Selena ever come up with the name Chase for the baby?"

Luke had a flashing, vivid memory of Selena impatiently telling him to cut to the chase that day she had come to his house. A reminiscent smile curved his lips. "The answer to that, dear brother, is classified information."

It was late. The house was silent. Chase was sleeping like . . . a baby. Luxuriating in the warm afterglow of delicious lovemaking, Selena curled into Luke's possessive embrace and brushed her mouth over his ear.

"I was only teasing earlier this evening," she murmured between tiny kisses and nips to his earlobe. "Like you, our son is handsome. But, unlike you, my love, he is not a devil."

"No?" Shivering in reaction to her caresses, Luke responded by trailing his fingers the length of her spine.

"No!" Selena replied on a gasp of pleasure. "Since he is the direct result of our love, I think of Chase as our little Christmas angel."

Tilting his head to look at her with devilish intent, Luke grinned and said, "In that case, what do you say to the idea of getting to work on producing a girl for next Christmas?"

The night, and Luke's hungry mouth, registered Selena's eager agreement.

* * * * *

WRITTEN IN THE STARS

**Star-crossed lovers?
Or a match made in heaven?**

Why are some heroes strong and silent . . . and others charming and cheerful? The answer is WRITTEN IN THE STARS! Coming each month in 1991, Silhouette Romance presents you with a special love story written by one of your favorite authors—highlighting the hero's astrological sign! From January's sensible Capricorn to December's disarming Sagittarius, you'll meet a dozen dazzling heroes.

Sexy, serious Justin Starbuck wasn't about to be tempted by his aunt's lovely hired companion, but Philadelphia Jones thought his love life needed her helping hand! What happens when this cool, conservative Capricorn meets his match in a sweet, spirited blonde like Philadelphia?

Take 4 bestselling love stories FREE

Plus get a FREE surprise gift!

proudly presents
the long-awaited ''prequel'' volume of

★ **LOVE AND GLORY** ★

by
LINDSAY McKENNA
Dawn of Valor

In the summer of '89, Silhouette Special Edition premiered three novels celebrating America's men and women in uniform: LOVE AND GLORY, by bestselling author Lindsay McKenna. Featured were the proud Trayherns, a military family as bold and patriotic as the American flag—three siblings valiantly battling the threat of dishonor, determined to triumph . . . in love and glory.

Now, discover the roots of the Trayhern brand of courage, as parents Chase and Rachel relive their earliest heartstopping experiences of survival and indomitable love, in

Dawn of Valor, Silhouette Special Edition #649.

This February, experience the thrill of LOVE AND GLORY—from the very beginning!

DV-1